Wish You the Best

Jay W. Rose

MILTON & HUGO L.L.C.
4407 Park Ave., Suite 5
Union City, NJ 07087, USA

Website: *www. miltonandhugo.com*
Hotline: *1- 888-778-0033*
Email: *info@miltonandhugo.com*

Ordering Information:
Quantity sales. Special discounts are granted to corporations, associations, and other organizations. For more information on these discounts, please reach out to the publisher using the contact information provided above.

Library of Congress Control Number:		2024901571
ISBN-13:	979-8-89285-176-3	[Paperback Edition]
	979-8-89285-177-0	[Hardback Edition]
	979-8-89285-178-7	[Digital Edition]

Rev. date: 05/23/2024

To my husband who has been very supportive of my writing journey.
Thank you for your unconditional love and support.
To my family and friends. Thank you for everything!

PROLOGUE

I watched him walk towards me as I listen to the sound of the rain hitting the roof of my car. Every step he took made my stomach turn; I knew what this was about when he asked to meet up. I watched as he took his right hand out of his pocket to open the car door, he sat in the passenger seat, let out a big sigh, and finally he took his red hood off his head. We sat in silence for a minute before he finally opened his mouth to speak but he hesitated and closed them right back.

In my head I thought, "dear Lord please just say something". But I sat there quietly with my head down just like his. We listened to the sound of the rain and the static coming from the radio. I wanted to tell him that I know, I've known for so long and if it makes him feel any better, it hurts me just as much. I could hear him breathing heavily, I know he's trying to gather the courage to say it out loud.

"I need to confess something…to tell you something" he finally said, quietly while keeping his head down. His hands were fidgeting with his car keys, and I could tell from his tone how scared and nervous he must feel. But I let it go, and I let him go at his own pace.

"You have no idea how awful I feel about this and saying it out loud makes me feel dumber, but I need to tell you." He cleared his throat as he finally lifted his head, but he wasn't looking at me. He was watching the windshield wiper as it continues to wipe off every rain drop even though it's pointless because the rain doesn't seem like it will let up anytime soon. I guess that's how we both feel inside too. We both know that no matter what we're about to say is just as pointless.

"I've been…I've been in love with you. It wasn't something that happened overnight but the more I got to know you, the more I felt strongly about you." He paused.

"I know it's wrong and I know this conversation will be pointless, but I needed to tell you. I'm sorry that my timing is wrong. But I can't watch you walk down that aisle in two weeks without telling you how I've felt. It's selfish, I know, but I have to tell you." He shook his head; I looked over to see that his eyes were turning red, and tears were starting to build up.

I took a few breaths before saying anything back. I knew how he felt but I didn't think that I was right. I know that he's waiting for me to say something, perhaps he thinks I might get angry and call him selfish, which he is, and I can't believe that this is happening now. But I gathered the courage to look at him and say, "I know...I've known for a while".

The look on his face will forever be painted in my head. He wasn't surprised that I knew, he looked apologetic.

"I knew but I didn't say anything... I didn't know what to say. But I know, it was no secret."

He turned his head towards me and looked me directly in the eyes, when he said, "I love you.".

TWO MONTHS TO GO

"Natalie! Come on! Just one more!", my friend Jade likes to push my limits, but in a good way. We've known each other since preschool and that's why I chose her to be my maid of honor. I'm an only child, I never knew what it was like to have a sister or sibling for that matter. Tonight, is different, we're in the middle of Nashville celebrating my bachelorette weekend with my two other bridesmaids. I can feel the "bride to be" tiara on my head getting tighter the more I drink, my "I'm getting f***ing hitched" sash keeps sliding off my shoulders as I try to chug a beer that I'm almost positive Jade contaminated with vodka because it tastes horrid.

"Okay! Okay! Give me a minute because I feel like I'm going to…" then I started gagging and rested my head on the bar table. My friends Alli and Sam were taking turns rubbing my back. Sam went to grab water from the bar while Jade continued to rile me up.

"Girl, you're about to get fucking married! That's right, throw up now because you're going to be the same man forever and ever and ever…" Jade used a very teasing and intimidating tone, but lucky for her I'm too worried about throwing up in front of strangers so I'm holding my mouth together.

We finally made it out of the bar, Alli kept wiping my face, I didn't realize how sweaty I was. I sat on the curb while we waited for our Uber, Jade is in the middle of the street, dancing and screaming, "my sister is getting fucking married!!! You boys lost your chance!" as she pointed at random obvious single men who walked pass her.

I already know how bad this headache is going to be when I wake up tomorrow but I'm okay with that, because isn't the point of a bachelorette getaway to live freely and wild, I mean…to an extent, before you spend

1

the rest of your life with the same person? I can feel my heart pounding and my head, probably from the alcohol but also the idea of being with the same person made me feel anxious. But I love Jake, he's been amazing to me, he takes such good care of me, and most of all he's been very patient with my mood swings. Jake and I met on our first day of college. I met one of his friends in one of my classes then one thing led to another I met Jake and we have been inseparable since.

I have never doubted his love for me, he has been through a lot and so have I. But together we were able to overcome everything and make a life together. We moved into our first apartment in Philadelphia after we graduated school. Jake grew up in Philadelphia and I'm from Woodbridge, Jersey. Jake got a job as an accountant, and I got a job as a social worker for orphaned children. Together we slowly decorated our apartment and hosted so many New Years Eve parties. Jake doesn't complain much about anything. He is very comfortable with letting me know when he's frustrated, upset, or overwhelmed. And I learned to do the same. We communicate everything with each other.

Jake proposed to me the day of graduation. We decided to have our wedding two years after he proposed to save up and to give us time to properly plan our wedding. Obviously, I said yes because I knew that he is the one for me and we have such a bright future together. I've known his friends for a while now too and honestly, sometimes I spend more time with him and his friends than I do with Jade, which she absolutely hates. I am comfortable around his friends; they've seen my messy hair first thing in the morning, and I've seen them passed out in my bathroom, so we call it even. But what I like the most about my relationship with his friends is that I feel like I know what it's like to have brothers who looks after me and tease me, endlessly. Jake is an only child too, so we don't know what it's like to have siblings, but our friends make up for it.

"He's here!!" as Jade ran towards a black Honda. Alli and Sam helped me get in the car. Of course, I had to sit next to the window in case I started barfing my guts out, which happened moments after our Uber started driving. Sam was holding my hair to keep it away from my face, so I didn't vomit all over my hair. Sam has always been so caring and very protective of me too. I know I can trust her with my life. Alli is the "baby" of our friend group, but she's always been one who can come up with the most logical solution to any problem we might have.

I could feel my eyelids getting heavier by the second, the wind felt nice against my face. I fell asleep before we could make it back to our Airbnb.

God damn, my head hurts so much, I need to go to the bathroom but I'm afraid if I move, I'll throw up. I lifted my legs towards my chest and laid on my right side, right now, this is the only position that doesn't make me feel sick to my stomach. I closed my eyes briefly then I heard my phone vibrate, it was a text from Jake.

How's it going? You laying on your right side with your knees against your stomach yet?

He knows me very well. Jake knows how I get when I drink too much because he's seen it over a million times. I tried to respond back but just moving my fingers to respond back made me nauseous. I haven't heard anything from the kitchen or living room, so I feel better knowing that my girls are just as bad as I am right now.

I finally woke up from my fifth nap, I didn't have anything to eat or drink other than the water bottle that I'm assuming, Alli left on my bedside table. I took a sip of water, and finally had the energy to get up and use the bathroom. I looked in the mirror and saw the horror as I stared at my reflection. Picture this, messed up hair from leaning my head out of the car window the whole ride back, my make up from last night is all over my face, and my shirt is no longer white. Pretty sight, huh?

I went into the kitchen and found Jade with her head on the kitchen counter.

"Good morning my sweet friend" I tease Jade. She listed her left middle finger.

I looked at the time and realized that it is now 2pm on a Sunday. We had a lot of fun last night. I cleaned up a bit, got showered and everything. Then I decided to finally FaceTime Jake.

"Hello, my beautiful fiancé. Did you have fun last night?" Jake asked.

"Jade" I responded with a little chuckle and shook my head.

"Oh… so you had a *fun* night." Jake knows how Jade and I can be when we're together, especially when alcohol is involved.

"Yeah, I don't remember much of last night, but I think it was fun."

"Well, I'm glad you did. You deserve the break, but don't forget you're almost a married woman" Jake teased.

"I can't wait to come home. I miss you."

"I miss you too, I'll see you tomorrow. I love you."

We hung up, I love Jake. He's such a kind man and I'm glad that we get to start a new chapter of our lives together. He doesn't make me feel bad when I tell him I need some alone time or when I want to spend time with my friends. He's always been so supportive and loving. I'm lucky I ended up with him.

That was the worst flight ever! Our connecting flight from Dallas to Philadelphia was pushed back five times! When we finally boarded our plane, somehow our entire group was put in different sections. I was stuck between a screaming child and a man who had no idea that arm rests exist. We finally got our luggage and headed for the exit. Jake was standing right outside with an iced caramel macchiato in his hand.

"You look wonderful" Jake said as he pushed my hair out of my face.

"I missed you" I said to him. I gave him a kiss and a hug then hopped in his car.

I watched Jade, Allie, and Sam hop in separate Ubers as we parted our ways after a long and memorable weekend together.

Driving through Philly is a nightmare, but I felt at home and comfortable by the fact that Jake is sitting right next to me. I told him everything that we did over the weekend. Since the world is against me today, we were stuck in traffic for a while, so I showed him all the pictures and videos that I took over the weekend.

After what felt like a ten-hour drive from the airport, we finally pulled into our apartment complex garage. Jake carried my luggage for me while I opened the front door. Oh, how much I missed our little apartment. Chelsea came running from the corner when she heard me call for her. Chelsea is a golden retriever that Jake and I adopted the year after we graduated college. We live on the 5th floor of an apartment complex in South Philly. I don't mind the city, I like watching the city lights from our little balcony, I love our little family. I don't know what I did to deserve this life, but I am grateful for it.

ONE MONTH TO GO

Four more weeks!! Four more weeks until all the planning, stress, and anxiety is over! Four more weeks until I get to walk down the aisle and marry the most important person in my life. I'm not going to lie; the last 8 months of planning has been stressful, but I intend for this to be my only marriage, so it is what it is. I just got home from my final dress fitting, my dress fits like a glove. Everything is slowly coming together. Jake has been very supportive through all the process. He even accepted that our office space has turned into my personal storage room for our wedding, he knows how to comfort me when he can tell that I'm beyond overwhelmed.

Tonight, is the second Saturday of the month. Every second Saturday, Jake and I host a game night with our friends. Usually, our night ends with some passed out on the couch, Jake usually has to wake me up from the couch and walk me back to our room by midnight, and a whole bunch of mess in the kitchen as if we're all still in college. But we're not, we're in our late 20's but we still try to keep our college selves proud.

The doorbell rang, Jason, and Ty walks in with cases of beer in their hands. Shortly after, the doorbell rings again. I looked through the peephole and found Jameson standing outside, also with a case of beer in his hands.

"Hey Nat, good to see you" Jameson greeted me as he entered our home.

"Come on in, Jake, Jason, and Ty are out on the balcony" I held the door open for Jameson.

Jameson and Jake have been inseparable since they were in middle school. Jameson moved to Pennsylvania when he was in 6th grade. The

5

story is that Jake accidentally sat at the peanut free table by himself then Jameson walked up to him and told Jake that it was nice to have another friend at the table. Jake has always been severely allergic to peanuts, Jameson was not. But Jameson stayed and for years told Jake that he is allergic to peanuts too. The truth is that Jameson didn't have the heart to tell Jake the truth. It was a cute little story but a start of a great friendship.

"So, how was your trip? Nashville, right?" Jameson asked as he cracked open a beer.

"Oh yeah, it was fun, I may have drunk a little too much." Then I told Jameson the story about me being halfway out the car window while I threw up all over downtown Nashville.

Jameson and I have always been able to get along, in fact, I consider him one of my closest friends now. Jameson is always around when we need help moving furniture, moving apartments, or to watch Chelsea when we go away. We talked in the kitchen for quite a while, we didn't realize how long we were talking until Jake and the guys walked in the kitchen.

"Oh, so the party is in the kitchen!" Ty teased as he raised his beer in the air. Ty thinks that he's still 23 sometimes. He's always been the life of the party. Jason has always been the quiet one but after a couple drinks, he turns into a chatter box and usually the reason why we can never get through a game without interruptions.

The rest of the group later showed up, Andrea, Sam, Leslie, Sean, and Joe all came not too long from each other. We started the night with a game of *Picture This,* then we switched to drunk Uno, which did not last very long after Ty won two rounds in a row. Our night slowly turned into a little karaoke party. Our neighbors surprisingly have never complained about us, the neighbors below said they can't hear us from their apartment, and our next-door neighbors says they're living vicariously through Jake and me.

After a while, the girls were all gone and we were left with me and the guys, which is typical. I decided to go out to the balcony and take a little break from drinking and Ty and Jason's karaoke battle. I heard the sliding door open and close behind me, I thought that Jake had come out to take a break with me but to my surprise it was Jameson.

"They're doing it again" Jameson shook his head as he chuckled.

"You know we can never have a successful game night" I smiled, typically our game nights last at least three hours then it turns into a circus show by Ty and Jason.

Jameson and I stood next to each other in silence as we watched the city lights and car drive by. It was quiet and peaceful.

"So, four more weeks huh?" Jameson said.

"Four more weeks, I can't wait for August 19th", I responded.

"Jake's a lucky guy to have someone like you... How many girls would let their man and his friends turn their house into a club once a month?" Jameson looked at me with a smile and a soft laugh.

"Oh, you know I don't mind. You guys are always welcome here. Plus, we're all going to grow old together so I might as well accept my faith", I said as I looked back at the sliding door. I could see Ty and Jason finally sitting on the couch, I'm pretty sure that Jake fell asleep on the other side of the couch, but I can't see him from where I'm standing.

"You know I almost met the perfect woman. But I screwed it up."

"What?? When? How come?", I was surprised because this is the first time I'm hearing about this.

"Oh, it was a while ago. I went back to the same spot a year later, but she wasn't there then the next time I saw her, she was already with someone else so I just kind of let it go."

Before I could ask more questions, I heard the sliding door behind us open. I turned and saw Jake. He came over and wrapped his arms around me, I know this look, if I don't get him to bed, he's going to pass out standing. I walked him back to our room. I turned my head to look at Jameson, but his back was turned. It sounds like whoever that person was still makes him upset. Maybe I'll get the full story some other time.

The next day, I woke up surprisingly with no hangover. Jake was still asleep, so I slowly and quietly got up to get ready. I walked out to the kitchen to clean up the mess from last night. Ty and Jason were both passed out on the couch. I was able to clean around them, they're both too deep in their sleep. I walked around to see if Jameson was still around, but it looks like he already left. I made myself some coffee and sat on the balcony for a while. I'm still wondering who the girl was, we all went to the same college, and I don't remember him bringing anyone around or talking to anyone throughout college.

I heard someone moving around so I went inside and made some breakfast before cleaning the rest of our mess. Jake came out to say good morning, gave me a quick kiss, then he bolted to the bathroom. I could hear him throwing up, but I wasn't surprised. Ty made himself the bartender last night so who knows what he was making and what he gave to Jake. Ty also got up, had breakfast then left to go home. Then there was me, I put on my headphones then proceeded to clean the rest of the house. "Who is she?", I asked myself as I continued to vacuum the living room. Why am I so curious about this girl?

THREE WEEKS TO GO

"Oh, you should be a model!" said Annette, my seamstress. I get to take my wedding dress home today. I couldn't stop looking at it, it's like it was made just for me, which was surprising because we found my dress buried in the back of the clearance rack at the bridal shop. Since our wedding is in mid-August, I decided to get out of my comfort zone and went for a strapless dress covered in tiny white pearls and jewels. The train is not too long but Annette did trim part of it to make it lighter on me. My veil is simple and goes all the way down to my waist. I get teary eyed just thinking about walking down the aisle and seeing Jake at the end of it.

"Well, now I just have to make sure that I stay this size for the next five weeks" I said with a little laugh.

"You know you won't but stay away from carbs and sweets until the August 19th" says my soon to be mother-in-law. Jeanine is a nice lady, she's very charismatic, but you can tell that she grew up in a $3.1 million dollar home. How do I know this? She never fails to mention it when every chance she gets. Jeanine is the only mother figure I have. My mom passed away when I was 10, my dad remarried when I was only six years old, and we haven't had much communication since. My grandmother took me in after my mom passed then she passed away when I was 16. Jeanine is supportive and has been caring towards me since Jake first introduced me to their family.

"Yeah, well I have to meet Jake for lunch. Thank you so much Annette, for everything" I gave Annette a hug and walked out.

I started walking down the street, I was trying to get my phone out of my pocket when I bumped into a gentleman, "oh my gosh I'm so sorry" I apologized, I moved my hair out of my face and looked up.

"Young lady, you should be paying more attention in the streets!"

I looked up to find Jameson standing in front of me.

"Jameson! I'm so sorry, I wasn't paying attention, I was trying to get my phone out of my purse, but my bracelet got stuck on my belt, then my hair was all over my face, then I…"

"Hey, it's okay, are you good?" he cuts me off, I realized that I was doing my panic explanation, or as Jameson and Jake likes to call, "panlanation", they said that I get this panic tone and I start to talk fast when I'm in a panic.

"Yeah, I just picked up my dress, I don't have it because Jeanine is taking it home with her, but I am on my way to Giorgio for lunch with Jake, and I realize that I'm doing my that thing, I'm sorry", I said with a little sigh at the end.

"Well, I can walk with you, so you have time to get everything out of your system before you have lunch with Jake", Jameson offered.

We started walking over, the restaurant is at least a 20-minute walk from here, but it's a Tuesday and I highly doubt I'll get there on time if I took a cab or an Uber. I love Philly but I hate the traffic.

"So, are you going to tell me what's making you all…chaotic today?" he said that nicely.

"I'm just…we're three weeks away from the wedding and I keep having to request time off for work so I can meet with the vendors, and you know, all the last-minute prep and now I realize that I completely forgot to call our caterer back, oh crap", I put my head down and kept walking then Jameson took his right arm to push me back. I realized that I was about to walk into traffic.

"Well, you can't call the caterer or meet with the other vendors if you get yourself run over by an angry Philly driver", he looked at me with a little smile and let out a little laugh. I like this about Jameson. He's always been protective of me, like an older brother, which I've always wanted one since I don't have any siblings.

"Thank you, but you're right, I can't be a bride if I'm lying in the middle of Center City" I let out a nervous laugh. "Thanks for the company and making sure I stay in one piece before I have lunch with my fiancé", I said.

"I'm always here, now go and get yourself something nice to eat. Make sure that Jake puts it on his credit card! Tell him I said so!"

Jameson yelled as he continued to walk backwards. I started walking towards the front of the restaurant when I turned around and watched Jameson walk away. He had both his hands in his pockets as he crossed the street.

I walked into the restaurant to find Jake, oh thank goodness! The one person I've been wanting to see all day.

Jake stood up and gave me a kiss and a hug, then he pulled my chair out so I could sit down.

"You good?" he asked, he can read me well.

I started telling him about every phone call I had to make this morning, all the running around to get things together for the wedding, then I told him that I bumped into Jameson, so he walked me over to make sure that I didn't bump into anyone or any cars.

"Jameson was here?" Jake seemed surprised when he heard Jameson's name.

"Yeah, he didn't say where he was going. Why?" I asked curiously.

"Nothing, he told me that he wasn't going to be in town this week but maybe he just came home early, no biggie", Jake said.

Before I could ask where Jameson was, our food came. Jake got his chicken carbonara pasta and I got my usual butter noodles with lemon and parmesan cheese. Servers in Italian restaurants always looks at me weird when I tell them my order, but I don't care. We enjoyed the rest of our lunch. Jake said that he has some things to wrap up in his office so he would be home late. He's been trying to get everything out of the way so that we can both be home the week of the wedding and then we are heading to Cozumel for our honeymoon the following week.

Jake and I walked out together then he went back to his office, and I decided to walk the next 6 blocks to the florist to deliver our final payment for the wedding flowers.

As I walked down the busy streets of Philly, I couldn't help but wonder where Jameson was and where he was going. He was wearing a long black sleeve shirt and jeans which I now realize is a ridiculous outfit to wear in the heat of summer. Looking back at it, I realized that Jameson looked sad. He was telling jokes, but his eyes looked sad. I wonder what happened, but it's not for me to ask. Right now, I need to focus on not getting hit by a car and to deliver a $500 check to the florist.

THREE AND A HALF WEEKS TO GO

My boss has been kind enough to let me work from home for the rest of this month to get some paperwork out of the way. I have been having a hard time focusing at home since I've turned our office area into my storage room for the wedding, so I decided to go to a little coffee shop just three blocks from our apartment. It's been rainy and gloomy so I decided that an iced cold brew would lift my spirits. I set my stuff at a small table by the window where I can watch cars drive by and count the rain drops as they fall out of the sky. I put my headphones on and opened my laptop to get some work done. After a while I looked up to look out the window and noticed Jameson standing across the street.

He was standing across the street in the rain, our eyes met, and he slowly made his way towards the café. He walked in and headed straight to the counter to order his coffee. Once he got his coffee, he started walking towards me and asked if he could sit down, I said yes and moved some of my stuff out of his way.

"Hey", he said quietly and almost in a sad way.

"You have to stop following me around", I joked and took a sip of my coffee.

"Yeah, sorry, I stopped by your apartment, but I realize that it's 9am on a Friday", he didn't smile at my little joke, he seems serious today.

"Jake went to work early so he can get everything done before Monday", I waited for a response, but he sat there quietly.

"Are you okay? You seem…quiet", I followed.

"I was actually hoping to talk to you" he said in a serious tone.

"Oh, what's going on?" I asked.

"I… I don't know, I just wanted to talk to you. You're easy to talk to", he didn't let me ask why, he finished his sentence before I had the chance to ask why he wanted to talk to me.

"Well, what about?" I asked.

"But now I'm not too sure if I should tell you or not", he responded.

"Jameson, come on, you know I can't stand when people say they have something to say then take it back! Tell me, whatever it is I'm sure I can handle it", I teased.

"Do you remember about the girl I told you about during game night?", he said.

"Yeah, I was curious about that. Who was she? I don't remember seeing you with anyone when we were in school." I responded followed by a sip of coffee.

"I never told anyone about her, not even Jake. I think you're the first person I told that to", he said.

"Well, you didn't give me a lot of information, so I didn't have anything to report back to Jake", I said jokingly.

"I'm kidding, it's not my story to tell. But what did you want to talk about?" I followed.

"She was the one. But I was too afraid to say anything to her, so nothing ever came out of it. I was just her friend and nothing more, I just let myself do things for her without her asking and I didn't want anything in return."

"Everything about her was perfect. She was kind, sweet, she could talk politics without defending either side, she was just very open-minded and willing to listen to anyone and accepted their opinions without being defensive."

"She sounds like she would have been perfect for you, I mean you're the same way with others." I replied.

"Yeah, then one night when I finally had the courage to tell her how I felt, but she showed up with another guy and he introduced her as his girlfriend. Then after that it felt that I couldn't talk to her anymore." He stopped. I could see the regret, sadness, and envy in his eyes. He wasn't looking at me, he kept his eyes at his coffee and his hands.

"So, who was she? Do I know her, or have we been in the same room together? I'm pretty sure it was always us and Jake…" I paused and thought of what I just said. I've never seen another girl hangout with our friend group throughout college. But no, it can't be, I'll just wait until he tells me more about her.

"You might know her", he finally lifted his eyes and looked into my eyes.

"I met her on the first day of school, she was there since the beginning", he said.

I sat there and tried to go remember if I ever saw him talking to another girl, but I don't think he ever introduced another girl to our friends. The longer I sat there to think the more frustrated I felt, why can't he just tell me? Then I looked up and noticed that he was staring at me. But not in a joking way like he usually does when he's trying to play tricks on me. His stare got deeper and his sad became sadder. The smile on my face slowly faded when I realized who he was talking about.

There's no way! I mean, Jameson and I have been very good friends and he's Jake's childhood best friend. What is he talking about? Is this a test? Did Jake put him up to this? I wanted to say all of this out loud, but I couldn't. Instead, I found myself staring back at him with my mouth slightly open and I probably had the most confused look anyone could possibly have on their face.

"What...who?" Those were the only words I could get out of my mouth.

"I know that you're marrying Jake and I'm happy for you, truly I am. But I needed to tell you about this girl because she was everything to me", he stood up and started to walk away.

"Are you serious Jameson? Or is this some kind of joke? It's not very funny", I said.

I sat there in silence, still probably looking confused as hell. What just happened? There's no way, I mean, I always thought that he cared for me because Jake is pretty much a brother to him. How can he say all of that and just walk away? What's his motive? What does he think I would say in response to his *story*? Do I tell Jake that his best friend of almost 20 years suddenly confessed that I was the one?

FRESHMAN YEAR

RINGGG!!! RINGGG!!! RINGGG!!!

I quickly shut my alarm off and got out of bed. It's the first day of freshman year of college, I need to look presentable just like everyone else. I got up to get ready for my 8 o'clock physics class. I looked up the distance from my dorm room to the science building, it's at least a 10-minute walk. It's 6:30 now so if I leave my room by 7 then I'll have time to stop for breakfast then find my classroom. I decided to go with my dusty blue dress, pair of white vans, I straightened my hair, and applied very light makeup. I don't want to look like I'm trying too hard, but I also want to make a good first impression, again, like every freshman girl in college.

I grabbed my brown backpack and headed for the door. I started walking to the cafeteria when I bumped into a tall kid, he looks like today is his first day as a freshman too. I hopped in line to grab a bagel and iced coffee. The line took a lot longer than what I was expecting. By the time I was able to pay for my breakfast I only had 10 minutes to find my class. I rushed to the science building, I found room 124 and grabbed a seat.

It's syllabus week but I've already planned out the entire year, like when I should be working on homework for each class, I already updated my planner with important due dates and exam days. I wasn't really paying attention then the guy next to me coughed and bumped my arm. I looked at him and he pointed to the front of the room with his eyes. Oh great, the professor was looking at me.

"Miss Natalie Anderson?" the professor said.

"Yes, that's me, I'm here…" then I slowly sunk myself into my seat.

"You should really pay more attention, *Miss Anderson*" the guy next to me said in a teasing way.

I let out a sigh and a smile. Oh, typical Natalie, I really should stop overthinking.

"My name's Jameson. *Mr.* Jameson Walsh"

"Funny, I'm…well you and everyone in this class knows who I am now" I responded.

"What's with all the planner stuff? It's the first day of school" Jameson said.

"Oh, I've always been like this, I like to be prepared, too prepared to even acknowledge my own name, apparently", I said.

"Well, there's 100 kids in this class, you're lucky you ended up sitting next to me" he said.

"Oh yeah? How come?", I was intrigued.

"I took AP physics in high school but I'm taking this class, so I have a guaranteed A this semester" he said.

We walked out of class together; I was expecting him to go the other way, but he started walking next to me.

"So, what's your schedule for the day?" Jameson asked.

"I have to find the math building; I have calculus at 10:15. How about you?" I responded.

"You know if we were in a movie, you'd think we were destined to meet each other" he said.

"How come?" I asked then he showed me his schedule.

It's nice that we have back-to-back classes together. At least it's one less class that I have to force myself to be friend someone new. My best friends and I went to different colleges, so I don't know anyone here. It's going to take me a while to make new friends. I like to stick to myself and spend most of my time reading or watching Netflix. Jameson is nice, I'm glad I met someone friendly. At least for now, until he learns that I pretty much live like a 90-year-old cat lady.

Jameson and I walked around campus for a bit. I learned that he moved to Pennsylvania when he was in 6th grade. I told him that I'm from Woodbridge but chose to stay in state so I can be a little closer to home which was a lie. Truth is, I'm too afraid of change and I was afraid that I'd be alone if I went somewhere far. Jameson seems to be a very confident person, he talks to anyone, he's the exact opposite of me. He seems to be a very open book type of person, I felt confident and comfortable enough to tell him a little bit about myself and childhood. We both have never been in a serious relationship. He said that the last girlfriend he had was in 10th grade but after that he was not interested in dating. He was a star varsity soccer player in high school. I told him that my ex and I broke up in the middle of our senior year because our career paths were very different and he wanted me to move to Chicago with him, which I was not ready for.

Before we knew it, we found our calculus class and sat next to each other. We were broken into smaller groups for a "get to know me" activity, I can't wait to do these 90 more times this week! Jameson and I ended in different groups, but I noticed that he kept looking back to see how I'm doing. I was not as sociable and humorous as Jameson, I could hear him making conversations with his group then there's me, I answer when someone directs their attention towards me.

After calculus I was about to head to the cafeteria to grab a to-go lunch and eat in my dorm, far away from people. I tried to say bye to Jameson, but he found a group of guys, so I guess that was it with my first day of school socialization. Everyone around me were talking to each other as if they've known each other for years. I quietly walked out, the last words that came out of my mouth were, "thanks", when someone held the door open for me. I proceeded to walk to get my lunch and anxious to get back to my room and hide until my 2pm literature class.

I grabbed food to go then started walking back towards my dorm, when I heard someone calling my name,

"Natalie!! Hey!"

I turned to see who was calling my name and to my surprise it was Jameson. He was with a group of guys; his one friend was walking with him towards me. I stopped and decided to wait, despite in my head I wish that I had pretended to not hear my name.

"Hey, I tried catching you after calculus, but you were already gone" Jameson said to me.

"Oh yeah sorry, you were talking so I didn't want to interrupt" I said apologetically.

"This is my buddy Jake, he was the one that I was telling you about, the peanut free guy", he wrapper his arm around his friends' neck which his friend jokingly tried to move away from him.

"Hi, I'm Natalie", I reached out my hand to shake Jake's hand.

"Yeah, I heard so much about you, I'm Jake, and despite what this guy may have told you about me, I swear I'm a decent person" Jake jokingly responded.

"Do you want to join us?" Jameson said, I could tell from his tone that he wants me to say yes.

I was having a dilemma in my head. Do I make an excuse so I can spend the rest of my afternoon alone? Or do I start over, in college, and make friends instead of being alone.

"Umm sure", I was surprised that I agreed to having lunch with a bunch of kids that I don't know at all.

Jameson introduced me to his friends; they were mostly guys which is very unusual for me because I am extremely shy around boys, and I have only had one best friend since elementary school. Jade is in Colorado for nursing but we still text constantly and stay in touch with each other. I miss her so much.

I found myself engaging in conversations and laughing at their jokes, I'm trying to remember their names, but Jameson and Jake are the ones that I can remember. "I should probably learn their names", I told myself. After an hour the rest of the group started to pack up to head to their next class, some of them are heading back to their dorms to take a nap. I almost felt sad that our lunch was over, I didn't think I would enjoy myself this much. Maybe college was the right choice for me to start over.

"So, where are you heading next?" Jameson asked.

"Probably head back to my room for a bit and rest" I said.

"Alright, well we'll probably be at the student center later, they're having first day of school barbeque. You should join us if you don't have plans later" Jameson offered, I don't think I have much of a choice but to say yes. He's been too nice to me today and has made my first day not as horrifying as I thought it would be.

"Yeah, I'll text you when I'm on my way" I said.

"It was nice to meet you *Miss* Natalie", Jake waved bye and started to walk backwards.

I started walking towards my dorm, I looked at my phone to check the time and oh crap! I have 5 missed messages from Jade. I told her I'd call her during lunch, but the time completely slipped my mind. I finally reached my dorm; I opened the door to see that my suitemate is not back yet. Samantha is nice but she is in the softball team, so she already has a group of people that she knows well. I opened my bedroom door, closed it behind me, then laid in my bed. I pulled my phone out to FaceTime Jade.

"Well…well…well…look who it is" Jade says teasingly.

"I'm so sorry!! The time slipped away, I was having lunch with some kids that I met earlier today" I told Jade.

"Oh? Natalie that's amazing!! I was thinking about you all day today! I was so worried that you'd eat your chicken salad alone…in your room…as always" Jade responded. She knows me very well; Jade knows that it's hard for me to socialize.

"So, who are they? What are their names? What did you talk about? I want to know *everything*!", she was too eager to hear about her best friend's not so terrible first day.

"Well, I embarrassed myself in front of 100 people in physics this morning because I didn't hear the professor call my name, more than once, but this kid next to me his name is Jameson and he kind of nudged me back to reality. Then Jameson and I also had calculus together after so we walked together and…" before I could finish the story, Jade cut me off.

"OH MY GOD!! NATALIE ANNE ANDERSON!!! You met a boy!!!!" Jade was too excited at the sound of a boy's name coming out of my mouth.

"So…tell me everything, was he hot? Is he single? Was he the one you had lunch with??" Jade was way too excited about this.

"Calm down! It's nothing like that, I think he could tell that I'm a very odd girl who needed some assistance on her first day. But yes, I had lunch with him and his friends".

Jade was shrieking. I think she's already planning my wedding and her maid of honor speech. After I told her everything, she finally calmed down and encouraged me to go to the barbeque later tonight.

"Natalie, you must go, okay? If you don't it will really break my heart. And I want to hear everything after!" Jade was not going to let this one go.

"Yeah, I told him I was coming, and I do want to see him and his friend Jake. Jake seems like a cool guy too, but he didn't talk much earlier."

"Well, Jameson or Jake, you have to go and send me pictures of them, so I know who to hunt down if I hear that someone breaks my best friend's heart".

"Jade it's nothing like that I swear, I just enjoy talking to them and finally making friends on my own".

"What are you wearing later?" Jade is not convinced that I'm only friends with Jameson and Jake.

"Oh, I was going to wear…"

"Let me guess, your ripped jeans, white t-shirt, and vans? Girl, no! Now yes to the jeans but you have those black long sleeves, and curl your hair, add more mascara too" Jade sometimes acts like she's my older sister even though I'm a year older than her.

"Yes, mom…I have to go, I want to get some rest, it's been a long day."

"Okay, but call me tomorrow, I want to hear everything! Love you Nat!"

"Love you too Jade Lynn."

We hung up and it was just me, silence, and this odd feeling in my stomach. I laid in bed and took a nap. Today has been a great day so far.

I got back from my 2pm literature class, no signs of Jess, I went to the bathroom and stared at myself in the mirror. I pulled out my curling iron and added some waves to my hair like Jade told me to. I fixed my makeup and got dressed. Am I trying too hard? What if seeing me this way might make the guys feel weird? Would they even notice? Ugh, I need to stop thinking too much. I grabbed my keys and phone and headed for the door.

I made it to the student center where they had music playing, there were people playing soccer and football, some people were sitting on the grass while chatting with their friends, there's too many people here. I tried to take small steps and looked around to see if I could find Jameson. I was starting to lose hope after five minutes, so I started to turn around when I heard someone call my name.

I finally found the group, I couldn't help but feel nervous, I still don't know any of them and I still don't see any girls in their group. I started walking towards them when Jake called my name and waved his arms in the air.

"Hey Nat, we thought you got lost" Jake said.

Nat?

"Yeah, sorry I didn't realize how big this event was going to be" I responded.

"No worries, come on over, we saved a spot for you!" Jake invited me to join him and his friends.

"Hey! There she is! Here, I put some marshmallow on this stick for you" Jameson handed me my marshmallows to roast.

I sat in between Jameson and Jake, I enjoyed listening to the guys joking around, it was refreshing to be a part of a group. After a while, it did get a little chilly, I started rubbing my arms and tried to pull my sleeves over my hands.

"Oh, here, take my sweatshirt" Jake gave me his gray sweatshirt that he was wearing. I noticed that he has a tattoo with coordinates on his left forearm.

"Thanks, are you sure?"

"Jake doesn't get cold; he's born with fire in his veins or probably the lack of nuts in his system" Ty jokingly said.

"Shut up Ty!" Jake responded and jokingly threw a marshmallow at Ty.

"I'm going to grab some soda; do you want anything Natalie?" Jameson offered.

"Actually, I'll go with you, I need to stretch out my legs anyway."

Jameson and I headed for one of the food trucks to grab some drinks. He seemed a little quiet, maybe he's getting tired, it is almost 9 o'clock.

"Jake's a good guy, he's an only child so he never had anyone to look after, younger siblings, I mean" Jameson said.

"Oh, yeah, it was nice of him to let me borrow this. Thanks for inviting me out tonight. To be honest, I probably would have grabbed another to-go meal and binge watch something on Netflix" I said.

Jameson smiled and acknowledged my appreciation. He seems a little tense, almost shy, which is unusual considering he was the most social person I met about 12 hours ago. Jameson went up to the food truck and grabbed a couple bottles of soda and water.

"I didn't know which kind you liked so I grabbed one of each" he said.

"I'll take a Sprite, thank you" I grabbed the bottle off his hand. I looked up at Jameson, but he wasn't looking at me.

"I didn't notice that scar on your index finger earlier" he said.

"Oh, it was from a stupid accident when I was about six. I thought that it was a great idea to try and take the chains off my bike but then my finger got stuck and it chipped my skin" I said while looking at my finger.

"Well, Miss Natalie Anderson, you are a very interesting person, and apparently made of steel", we started to head back with the rest of the group.

FRESHMAN YEAR MIDTERMS

It's almost noon, I'm waiting at our usual table for our daily lunch, some days Ty and Jason doesn't show up, they usually end up skipping lunch to take naps. Most days it's just me, Jameson, and Jake. There have been some days when it was just Jake and I, or Jameson and myself. Our group has been getting bigger, especially now that Ty and Jason have girlfriends. It's nice to not be the only girl some days. I have made some friends outside of our group too but it's hard to replace the first people who took me in on our first day.

"Hey, sorry I had to ask my professor some questions, so I didn't get to leave on time", it was Jake, and he looks a little stressed.

It is the week before midterms so every single student on campus pretty much has the same look on their face.

"It's all good, I wasn't here long. Is Jameson coming?" I asked.

"I don't know I haven't heard from him since this morning" Jake took a big bite of his burger and took a deep breath.

Jake is a nice guy, I found that we have a lot of things in common, but he is a bit more social than I am. Every time we're all hanging out together, Jake makes sure that I'm comfortable and he has gotten pretty good at reading my expressions and he can usually tell when my social battery is low. Jake and Jameson made up a word called, "panlanation", it's supposed to be "panic and explanation" mixed. I tend to explain too much when I'm in a panic or anxious. Jake and I became close with each other over the last few months. There have been nights when he comes over for a movie night when Jameson is not around.

Jake and I started eating our lunch, I took a bite of my pasta, then Jake reached to wipe the pasta sauce off my chin. Jake acts a lot like a big brother and so does Jameson, they're both not afraid to tell me when I look like a mess.

"I see you guys already started. How's everyone's day? Jameson said then sat in between Jake and me.

"Midterms man, why is this a thing?" Jake said as he shook his head.

"We didn't know where you were, I texted you earlier" I said.

"Yeah, I forgot to charge my phone last night, so it's been dead" Jameson responded.

Jameson was focused on his food, but he looked angry, I have been noticing that Jameson has not been as talkative lately. I wonder if the midterms are making him stressed. He also started two part-time jobs to pay his mom back for fixing his car last month. He has not been around as much lately because when he's not working as a bartender downtown on the weekends, he's at the library for the overnight shift, then classes the rest of the day. I really don't know when he sleeps.

The three of us quietly finished out lunch, Jameson said that he needed to run to take a quick nap. I was about to ask him if we're having our taco night tonight, but he got up and walked away in almost a hurry. Then it was just Jake and I, he grabbed my trash and tray to put away, I waited for him by the door before we headed back to our dorms.

"Are you doing anything later?" Jake asked.

"Umm I might go to the library after 5pm, but who knows how long I'll be there", I said.

"Hey Nat", Jake said.

"Yeah?"

"Nothing, I forgot what I was going to say" he said.

Jake usually will walk me back to the front of my building, it's really a sweet gesture, considering that his dorm is in the opposite direction of mine.

"Hey Nat, I'll join you later at the library. I have some studying to do too" he said.

"Sounds good, I'll text you when I get there" I responded.

We went our separate ways; I've been noticing lately that Jameson and Jake have been quiet when we hang out. I'm sure that the stress is finally catching up to them, they're both such easy-going people so it is noticeable when they're not being themselves. I pulled my phone out of my pocket as soon as I made it back to my room. I tossed my bookbag on my desk and laid in bed. Something about Jameson today was different, he didn't seem like he wanted to be around anyone. I decided to send him a text and asked if he'd be interested in meeting later before he has to go to work.

Meet by the tree at 6?

I texted and he immediately read it, but it took him three minutes to respond.

Sure.

"Sure"? That's it? That's what he was thinking about? I'm probably just overthinking but it has been almost a month since the last time Jameson actually spoke to me. Some nights I wonder if I did something that made him upset or maybe he's getting tired of hanging out with me. Ugh, who knows.

I took a short nap then grabbed my stuff to meet Jameson, I realized that I was walking faster than usual. Part of me was excited to see Jameson, it feels like it's been forever since the last time the two of us hung out. I finally made it to our spot but there's no signs of him. I sat there and thought about going inside to grab something to drink but I didn't want Jameson to get here and think that I ditched him. Ten minutes go by and he's still not here nor has he texted me to let me know when he's on his way.

I'm here. I texted.

No response and no read receipt, I decided to wait another ten minutes before I head over to the library. I was ready to give up when Jameson finally showed up. He seemed angry and not in the mood to talk at all. He sat next to me but didn't look at me.

"Is everything okay with you?", I asked.

He didn't say anything and kept his head facing the other way. I was starting to feel irritated, so I finally stood up.

"Well, if you're not going to talk then I guess I'll leave you to it", I said.

"Everything's great Nat, everything's *fine*", he said but his tone says otherwise.

I sit back down and looked at him.

"What's wrong?", I asked again.

"When were you planning on telling me?", he asked.

"Tell you what?", I responded.

"I'm not dumb Nat, I wish that you would have told me", his tone changed.

I'm really confused, tell him what exactly?

"I don't know what you're talking about. If you give me more details then I'd probably be able to answer it", I said to him.

"Just forget it, I have to go to work", he said.

Jameson got up to leave, he didn't stop to look back at me or apologize for his rude behavior. I stayed there until he was gone, I'm still very confused, I don't know what it is that he knows that I supposedly didn't tell him. I grabbed my bag and started to walk towards the library when Jameson stopped then put his head down. I rolled my eyes and kept walking as fast as I could. Jameson and I have never gotten into an argument, let alone a fight.

"Nat", I heard him call for me.

I kept walking, I'm making it known that I'm mad at him. Which is stupid because I don't know what he's talking about, but he won't say.

"Hey, Nat", I could tell from the sound of his voice that he's getting closer to me.

We came to a stop at the crosswalk, stupid street sign won't turn green fast enough. I crossed my arms across my chest and continued to look the other way as if I can't hear him.

"Okay, I get it. I'm sorry, I shouldn't have talked to you that way. I'm sorry", he apologized.

The light finally turned green, so I started to cross then realized that Jameson was walking beside me.

"Hey", Jameson said softly.

His eyes looked apologetic, and I don't think I can ever stay mad at him so decided to stop and acknowledge him.

"Will you *please* tell me what it is that you're upset about?", I begged.

"Nothing, it was stupid. I'm having a bad day, and I just took it out on you", he said.

"We both know that's bullshit Jameson but whatever", I started to walk away again.

"Nat wait please", he said as he grabbed my shoulder.

"So?", I waited for him to tell the truth.

"I…when were you going to tell me that you two are going out?", he asked, I'm still confused.

"Out with who? Can you please just tell me what it is instead of asking me questions that I don't know the answer to", I demanded.

"You and Jake, since when did you two started going out?", he finally said.

I looked at him with a confused look since last time I checked I wasn't going out with anyone let alone Jake.

"Me? And Jake? Where the hell did you get that from?", I confronted him.

"I heard from Ty and Jake earlier when they were talking, they thought I was asleep. So, is it true?", he confessed.

"So, you were eavesdropping your friends?", I said as I took a step back, crossed my arms, and looked at him in the eyes.

"No, I wasn't trying to, I was trying to take a nap when they walked in then I overheard one of them say your name, so I just kept listening", he said.

"Well, it's not true but if I was going out with Jake then why would it be such a big deal to you?", I said.

Jameson's face changed this time he actually did look mad.

"It's not a *big deal* to me Natalie. I don't care who you want to go out with but…", he paused.

"You know what? Never mind, have fun at the library", he shook his head and walked away.

What the heck just happened?

SOPHOMORE YEAR

This year I was lucky enough to get a single room suite, Jess decided to rent an apartment with some of the girls from her softball team and I was perfectly fine with having a place all to myself.

"Alright, now *this* should be the last box" Jake said as he wiped the sweat off his face.

Jake offered to help me move into my new suite, this year Jake, Jameson, and I are all in the same building which was comforting.

Jake and I saw each other a couple of times this summer, he came to visit me in Woodbridge, and I spent a weekend in Philadelphia with him and his mom. Jake's mom was kind enough to let me stay with them. We didn't get to see Jameson as much this summer, he was busy with working and helping his mom take care of his younger brother. Jameson comes from a single parent household, so he watches his younger brother while his mom works overnights at the hospital. We facetimed a couple of times and of course stayed in touch with each other. We haven't heard from Jameson to let us know when he's moving back.

Jake stuck around to help me unpack my boxes and move furniture around my room. Once we were done, we headed to the cafeteria to grab a quick bite before we went back to our rooms to organize our things. Still no signs of Jameson, Jake says that maybe he plans on moving back tomorrow. Jake and Jameson are roommates this year, so Jake says he'll be around to help Jameson once he decides to show up.

I went back to my room to finish unpacking and organize my things. I kept checking my phone to see if Jameson texted me back, I had 4 messages from Jade. She joined a sorority last year so she's excited to move into her sorority home this year. I sent Jade a picture of my suite to get her opinion on my room decors.

Hey, what time are you coming? Was my last text to Jameson this morning.

After making my bed, I decided to lay down for a bit when I received a text from Jameson.

Hey, sorry, been busy. I'm moving in tomorrow, gotta help mom with some stuff first.

Jake says that Jameson's mom was laid off from her job at the hospital so she's working two part-time jobs right now. Jameson is such an amazing son for helping his mom and brother, he's always put his family first, and I respect that about him.

This year is a little different, this time I'm not as anxious, I'm not afraid to leave my room and be around other people, and I have friends. But something tells me that this year will be different. Something is making me feel anxious, excited, and happy to be here, or maybe someone. My first year was beyond what I imagined it would be. I think I might be falling for someone.

It didn't take long for my second year to suck the life out of me. There's more pressure this time around. I no longer feel the need to put myself together, I usually show up in a sweatshirt and leggings with iced coffee in my hands. I barely see the guys anymore since our schedules are the opposite of each other. I do get to hang out with Jake most nights, we typically meet up at the library and stay until closing time. We've grown much closer with each other lately; Jade says that Jake has a crush on me but that's just Jade. She desperately wants me to have a boyfriend.

I haven't been in a serious relationship since high school, it would be nice to have someone, but I haven't had any interest in anyone. Sure, I've seen guys on campus who are attractive, but I can never picture myself going out with any of them, let alone for them to approach me first. I've never been a "dating" type of person, I think that after watching my mom struggle after my dad left us when I was six, it pretty much traumatized me. I've always had the mindset that if my own father can leave me for someone else, then anyone can. Hence, I never bothered to jump from one guy to another, I want to find one person and spend the rest of my life with that person. It's wishful thinking I know, but a girl can only dream, right?

"What?", I said jokingly to Jameson. We're in the library; he's sitting across from me, and I noticed that he has been staring at me for a while. Jake had a group project so he went to meet with his group, Jameson had the night off so he asked if we could go to the library together.

"Huh?", he said, confused.

"Is there something on my face? Or something wrong? You've been staring at me, it's starting to creep me out", I teased.

"Oh sorry, I just spaced out", he responded with a smile.

"Hey Nat, hypothetically, if we weren't friends, would you go out with me?" he asked very randomly.

"What? What do you mean?", I responded.

"You know, like right now, if we didn't know each other and I approached you and asked for your number, would you give it to me?", he asked.

"I mean, maybe, I think, I don't know", I responded.

"What, I'm not good looking enough for you?", he said.

"No, it's just hard to think about that because we've known each other since our first day. But I mean I would if I didn't know you. What made you think that?", I said, I was confused and taken aback by his question. At first, I thought he was joking but I can see now that he's being serious.

"Nothing, I just wondered why after a year and a half of college, you haven't gone out with anyone", he said.

"I don't know, I guess no one really has asked me for my number or bothered to talk to me", I responded. Jameson is right, I haven't gone out on a single date since we started college.

"Probably because people see you with Jake all the time and thinks you're together. It can be intimidating to a guy to approach a girl, especially if we see them with the same guy almost every day", he said.

I guess that makes sense, I never really thought of that. I do spend a lot of time with Jake but it's not like Jake and I are interested in each other. Sure, I find him attractive, but I don't think Jake sees me as anything other than a friend.

"Well, I don't think my love life is a part of our homework, so...", I said to get out of this conversation.

"You're right, I'm sorry, I have no business. It's just I care about you and…nothing, let's get back to it, shall we?", Jameson said as he pulls out another notebook out of his bookbag.

Jameson and I were heading back to our dorm when I missed a step outside of the library and almost fell, luckily, he caught me in time, so I didn't hurt myself.

"Are you alright?", Jameson asked, I could hear the concern in his voice.

"Yeah, I'm okay, thank you", I responded.

"See, if we didn't know each other and you happen to trip and almost fall over. This would be a romantic first meeting, wouldn't it?", he said.

"Haha! Okay Romeo", I laughed then playfully rolled my eyes at him.

I could feel Jameson's hand on my back as we continued to walk down the stairs and sidewalk, he knows how clumsy I can be, so chances are I'll probably trip over nothing again. Jameson walked me to my door; we said good night and parted ways.

I'm lying in bed and all I can think about is my conversation with Jameson earlier. Maybe he's right, but it's also not a priority, I guess if it happens, it happens but why should I stress myself out over it? I tried closing my eyes but every time I do, I see one person. The one person who's been there for me all along. Maybe I am interested in this person, but do I want to risk losing one of the most important people in my life? Ugh, I can't stop my head from spinning.

Hey, are you okay?
It was a text from Jameson.
Yeah, why? I texted him back.
I'm sorry if I put you on the spot earlier.
Wanna grab a late snack? He followed.
Sure. I responded back.

I quickly grabbed a sweatshirt and threw my sneakers back on to meet Jameson for a late-night snack, I looked at the time and realized that it is almost midnight. I met Jameson in the lobby of our building then walked out together. It's crazy how different the campus looks like this late at night. It's more peaceful and not as intimidating. I looked up and noticed that tonight is a full moon, and all the stars are out. Jameson and I grabbed some snacks from the grab-and-go bar then we headed out to our usual spot, but some people beat us to it, so we found a spot out in the lawn. Jameson took his jacket off and laid it on the grass for me to sit on.

"You ever wonder what it's like to be up there?", I pointed to the sky.

"I have been on a plane so not really", he responded but I could tell that he was being sarcastic.

"No, I mean, what it's like to be as far up as the stars. It's probably quiet, peaceful, and stress free", I said as I jokingly nudged him with my elbow then we were followed by silence.

"Hey, I'm sorry about earlier, I really didn't mean to put you on the spot. I don't want you to think that there's anything wrong with not having a boyfriend. I do admire that you're not in a rush, that's all", he said sincerely.

"It's really okay, you don't have to keep apologizing", I reassured him.

"But sometimes I do think about it. Like when will I find *that* person, you know?", I followed.

"When my dad left, I still remember how hurt my mom was. I remember how she tried to act like everything was okay because of me, she probably didn't think I knew what was going on. She told me every day, "Dad will be back, honey", I think she was saying that to reassure herself, not me", I continued.

"I've just been cautious about falling in love with anyone. If I find someone, I want it to last. I don't want to go through breakups and start over every time, I don't want to cry myself to sleep for years like she did", I said.

"You're not her and not all men are like him", Jameson responded as he turned to look at me.

"I do hope that you find what you're looking for and I hope that when you do find it, that you're happy", he said and gave me a smile.

"Well, that was a deep one" I sighed.

"How about you? Has any girl been on your mind lately?", I asked.

"Not really, I'm in the same boat. I'm not in a rush to be with anyone right now", he said.

I looked at Jameson and our eyes meet. I took a bite of ice cream then leaned back to get a better look at the stars. For a moment my head wasn't spinning, I wasn't sad about my father leaving then my mom passing. I was content, I felt at peace. I realized moments later that we were sitting really close to each other, and our hands were touching but maybe Jameson didn't notice it either or he just doesn't care. Then, suddenly I felt his pinky grab mine almost like we're doing a "pinky swear". I didn't move my hand, I felt comfortable and safe. With each minute that passed before we know it his right hand was over mine.

I could feel my face starting to turn red and butterflies in my stomach. Jameson adjusted himself closer to me. We're both looking up at the stars, pretending like it's completely normal for us to be this close. We still haven't said a word to each other, I keep trying to think of things to say, to talk about, but this very moment seems to speak for itself. Is this why he was asking if I'm interested in anyone? I tried to convince myself not to read too much into it.

We have been really good friends since we started school last year so we're both really comfortable around each other. I noticed the clock tower says it's already pass midnight, but I didn't want to ruin this moment. Deep down I wished for time to stay still, my heart was beating faster and faster, but I didn't want to make it too obvious, so I took my hand and brushed a piece of hair off my face. When I put my hand back down, I realized that Jameson had moved his hand away too.

"I guess we should head back", Jameson whispered.

He's right but part of me was disappointed that we have to leave, I didn't want this moment to end. I looked at him and nodded my head in agreement. Jameson helped me up and our eyes immediately locked. It felt that everything and everyone around us suddenly froze. Suddenly the sound of people walking, talking, and even the sound coming from the crickets disappeared. It's just us staring into each other's eyes, not saying a word. He took a step closer to me and I let him. He takes his right hand to my face and slowly he got closer, is this it?! I froze, I could feel the butterflies in my stomach, my face started to feel warmer and warmer. I knew what was going to happen, but I didn't know how I'm supposed to react.

The moment he was close enough, too close to me, he stopped and pulled away. Did I do something wrong? Did I not react the right way? He gently brushed my hair off my face before letting go with a smile on his face. I smiled back and tried to divert my attention elsewhere. Jameson cleared his throat and tried to look away too. Jameson grabbed my things and gently placed his hand on my back to guide me. We started to walk back to our dorm, I kept my head down and looked around while we're walking then I quickly glanced over at him, he was smiling. Jameson insisted on walking me all the way back to my room even though his room is in the opposite direction from mine. We finally made it to my door; I kept my arms crossed across my chest while Jameson slowly took his hand off my back. I looked up to find that he was staring right at me. We didn't say anything for a moment.

"Good night, Natalie", he said as I unlocked the door and started to walk in.

I turned and responded, "good night, Jameson".

I closed the door behind me, my heart felt like it was going to jump out of my chest. I wanted to check to see if he's still standing out there, but I didn't want him to think that I'm too desperate. I smiled and went into my room; tonight was a good night.

I laid in bed, but I couldn't help but replay *that* moment over and over in my head, I smiled every time I pictured him closer to me. Every time I closed my eyes all I could see was his face and the way his eyes met mine. What am I doing? Am I falling for him?

NOW: STILL THREE WEEKS TO GO

After Jameson got up and left, I watched him walk away, I watched him until he was gone. I keep thinking back to our early college days, how did I not see it then? Jameson was right, he was there all along. From our first day to our last, he never failed to show up and help me without being asked. But was I that dumb that I didn't see his efforts? Sure, we had some moments when we were in college, but nothing ever happened, and he never told me how he felt. There were times when I thought maybe he liked me, but he shut me out. Maybe I am *that* oblivious. I feel so guilty but what am I doing? I am getting married in three weeks to our best friend. Jake has always been by my side, sure I met him because of Jameson but what am I supposed to do with this information that his best friend just confessed?

I looked down and noticed that I had three missed calls and a text message from Jake, *"hey babe, I'll be home a little late tonight. I'll pick up food, is that okay?"*. What am I doing? I have a man who is willing to give me the world despite my flaws. But I can't help but think about Jameson and the look in his face, his eyes were full of sadness and regret. How am I supposed to know that I've hurt him, if he never said anything to begin with? I mean, it has been five years since we graduated college. We spent four years together and not once did he expressed that he liked me then, so why is he doing this now? Ugh...my head is spinning.

I can't help but wonder if I fell for the wrong person. But, no! No! I chose Jake and he chose me! He's been by my side since the day we met and he has been nothing but kind, loving, and caring. Why would I want to throw away what I have for someone who didn't have the guts to say anything?! I hate Jameson for doing this, for making me doubt my decisions, for making me doubt the person that I am and the person that

I'm with. I'm getting married in three weeks! All I can do is wonder, "why", and how angry I am at Jameson for throwing this in my face then walk away! I can't read his mind, how was I supposed to know?

I look back in our pictures from our college days, every picture is the same, Jake, Jameson, and myself. It's always been the three of us. What do I do now? Jameson is Jake's best man, how is he going to stand next to his best friend knowing that he has been holding these feelings for years, and how am I supposed to walk down the aisle knowing that I have this guilt. But I shouldn't feel guilty, I did nothing wrong. I fell in love with Jake, and I said yes to being his wife and to stand by his side for the rest of our lives.

All I could do was pull out my phone and write a message to Jameson,

> *How can you be so selfish? For fuck's sake Jameson! I'm getting married in three weeks and you're throwing this in my face now?? What were you thinking? How was I supposed to know if you didn't say anything?? What did you think was going to come out of this big revelation of yours?! Am I supposed to leave YOUR best friend at the altar? Am I supposed to throw everything away because my best friend of almost a decade finally decided to tell me that he has feelings for me?? God, I'm so angry with you! I wish that you never said anything!*

I wrote it but didn't have the guts to send it. As much as I have every reason to be angry, what good is it going to do? What's done is done. I don't have anything to think about because I know that Jake is the one for me and I am going to marry him. I will walk down the aisle and say, "I do".

The more I thought about Jameson the more anxious I felt. I can't help but think that maybe I'm making a mistake by marrying Jake. What if I was meant to be with Jameson? This is one of those moments when I wish I could call Jade and she'll tell me what to do. But this is different, I need to figure this out on my own.

JUNIOR YEAR

The first half of this semester is killing me! I did join the creative writing club this semester and it has been helpful with getting my mind off things. Jake invited me to be his "plus one" at his fraternity formal this evening. I found a navy-blue silk dress and a shawl to wear over it in case I get cold. Jake joined a fraternity last year and he seems to really like it. Jameson is still working multiple part-time jobs, so he said that he doesn't have time to join any clubs. Jameson has been MIA most days, there are times when he will randomly show up to social gatherings or lunch but for the most part, we haven't heard from him as often.

I finally made it back to my dorm, I quickly grabbed a shower, and started to put myself together for Jake's formal. He's supposed to pick me up in an hour, so I quickly did my hair and makeup and put on my dress. This is the first time I've worn a formal attire since high school, I kind of like it, it's nice to be able to dress up and not think about writing my final paper for my writing class.

An hour goes by when Jake finally texted me that he is waiting outside. I walked outside and found Jake leaning on his car. He was wearing a black suit, brown shoes, and his hair sleeked back. I won't lie, he looks hot.

"Wow, you look amazing Nat" Jake complimented me.

"Thanks, so do you", I responded.

He walked around his car and opened the door for me, we got in his car and drove to the event. When we finally made it to the hotel, I was surprised to see how many people are here. I didn't realize that there were this many people in his fraternity and of course almost everyone brought a plus one.

Jake offered me his arm as we walked inside the venue together. I feel different, I haven't felt this way in a while, almost like a princess walking to a ball. When we got inside, I surprised to see Jameson, he was standing with Jason and Ty and I'm assuming their plus ones. I wonder who invited Jameson, I don't see anyone with him. As we got closer to the group, I noticed Ty and Jason were staring at me, they have never seen me in anything but a sweatshirt and leggings since the day we met. Jameson was looking at me too.

"Gentlemen, may I introduce to you, Miss Natalie Anderson. My girlfriend", Jake introduced me as if the guys don't know me.

"Well, well, well, you finally did it!" Ty said to Jake and gave him shook his hand very enthusiastically.

"Did this happen recently? Congrats guys!", Jason said.

"Umm, we've been going out for about three months now, right, Nat?" Jake responded.

"Yeah, about three months", I said.

Ty and Jason were all up Jake, teasing him for the most part. Then I looked at Jameson who has not said a word since we arrived.

"Hey", I said to Jameson.

"Oh hey! How have you been? I wasn't expecting to see you tonight" I said.

"Yeah, I have the weekend off and I'm good friends with Pat, so he invited me to come out", Jameson responded. Pat is the president of Jake's fraternity.

There was an awkward silence, Jameson continued to avoid eye contact, he would smile and let out a fake laugh as if he's listening to what Ty and Jason were saying. He seemed unhappy, almost angry.

"Umm, so how are things?" I tried to initiate a conversation.

"How are things? Well, let's see, I've been working almost every night, going to classes, haven't had much of a social life, and then I find out tonight that my best friends are boyfriend and girlfriend and didn't bother to tell me until now, I'm doing great Nat", Jameson said then he walked away.

Ty, Jason, and Jake all looked at me and then followed Jameson with their eyes.

"What was that about?", Jason said.

"I'll handle it, I'll be back", Jake said as he followed Jameson to the bar.

I stood there with Ty and Jason, I wasn't listening to what they were saying, I was watching Jake and Jameson from afar. I can't really tell what they're talking about, but Jameson is upset. I did realize that Jake and I haven't told Jameson about us, but he's been very unavailable lately so we never had the opportunity to tell him before we could tell the rest of the group. Jake asked me out about three months ago, we have been hanging out even when we're not in school. One thing led to another, Jake asked me out to dinner then expressed how much he liked me and asked me to be his girlfriend. We really didn't use any terms to describe us, we're dating but tonight was the first time that Jake has introduced me as his girlfriend to anyone.

Jake started to walk towards us, Jameson stayed at the bar with his head down, he still looks upset.

"So, is he mad about us?", I asked Jake.

"He'll be fine, he just needs some time to process. Anyway, I got you a drink", Jake handed me my drink. I could tell that Jake feels intense, but he doesn't want to show it.

The whole night I felt uneasy, and I could feel my heart beating out of my chest. I keep looking back at Jameson. He hasn't left the bar since he walked away and that was about an hour ago. I wanted to walk over and talk to him, but Jake said that it's best to let him cool off especially since Jameson started drinking. I tried to enjoy the rest of the night, Jake introduced me to his fraternity brothers, we danced a little, and had some food and drinks. At one point, I looked over to check on Jameson and caught him staring back at me.

"Do you need another drink?" I asked Jake.

"Um, I'm okay, do you want me to get you another?" he asked.

"It's okay, I'll be right back", I gave Jake a kiss and headed towards the bar.

I walked over to the bar and stood next to Jameson, I know I shouldn't, he probably doesn't want to talk to me.

"I'll take another Moscato, please", I said to the bartender.

I want to say something, but I don't know where to start. I grabbed my drink and was about to walk away when Jameson gently grabbed my arm to stop me from walking away.

"Nat, wait", he said quietly.

I looked at him, his head was down then he finally looked at me. Has he been crying? His eyes were red, and he looked really exhausted.

"I'm sorry, I shouldn't have yelled at you like that", Jameson apologized.

"You didn't yell at me, but it's okay. Thank you", I responded.

Then there was silence, I looked to see if Jake is watching us and sure enough, he was. I think he was worried that Jameson will cause a scene, but he seemed relieved to see us standing, in peace. Another moment passed when Jameson finally said something else.

"I'm happy for you and Jake, I know that you guys don't need my permission, I was just in shock, and I didn't handle my emotions well. I'm sorry", Jameson grabbed his drink and started to walk away before I could say anything.

"Jameson, wait", I stopped him.

"I'm sorry that you had to find out this way. We should have told you sooner but you've been kind of hard to talk to lately so I told Jake that it might be better if we told you in person", I explained.

"Yeah, thank you", he sighed and walked away.

I watched Jameson walk into the sea of people until I could no longer see him. I walked back to Jake and told him what Jameson said. Jake rubbed my back and kissed my forehead. I know that it's not easy for Jake to see Jameson this way, they've been brothers since they were kids. I feel guilty, I feel that I'm causing a rift between them, but Jake reassured me that, that's not the case, and that Jameson will come around again. We continued with our night; I ended up staying over at Jake's after the party.

We laid in bed; Jake immediately fell asleep. Meanwhile, I couldn't sleep, all I could think of was how sad and upset Jameson was. But I think that Jake is right, he just needs time to cool off and Jameson is very stressed out lately. Maybe I'll talk to him once he's ready. I hope that this doesn't end our friendship. Jameson has been a brother to me and one of my best friends, I would hate to lose him.

The following day, I grabbed my phone as soon as I opened my eyes. Should I reach out? Did he make it home? I barely slept last night. I kept thinking about the way Jameson was so hurt when he found out about me and Jake, the way he looked at me, and the way his voice sounded. I knew that it would upset him, but I didn't think he would be this upset. Maybe I should give him another day and let him cool off.

Moments later, Jake woke up, we both laid in bed, we didn't say a word for a while. I know that we were both thinking about our best friend and how our relationship hurt him. Jake eventually sat up, looked at me, and said good morning. Then he headed to take a shower and I stayed in bed. My phone kept buzzing, but it was all text messages from Jade, I haven't had the chance to tell her about last night. I wonder how long I have to wait before I can reach out to Jameson.

I stayed in bed and stared in the ceiling, completely ignoring my phone. All I could see was the look on Jameson's face. He looked so hurt, betrayed by his best friends. But what was I supposed to do? He hasn't been around, and he barely answered my texts. He has been very distant, and it felt that every time I tried to take one step closer to him, he would take three steps back away from me. The last time Jameson and I hung out with each other was last semester when we grabbed some ice cream and had an "intimate" moment. But after that night, Jameson never brought it up again, so I figured that we were both feeling sad that night.

"Pancakes or waffles?", Jake asked.

"Huh?", I responded.

I didn't realize that Jake was done in the shower, nor did I realize that he was talking to me.

"Any preference for breakfast?", he asked again.

"Pancakes, please", I said.

"Okay, stay in bed, I'll bring it over when I'm done", he said and gave me a kiss on my forehead.

Jake has been very kind and sweet. He's been the best boyfriend a girl could ask for; he takes really good care of me, and he's been very good at reading me. He knows when I need space and when I need him the most. I know that he's probably not too happy about last night either. Jake had told me that Jameson seems like he has been avoiding him since last summer. I feel guilty that I might be the reason that his best friend has stopped talking to him but what was I supposed to do? I don't think Jameson saw me as anything other than a friend. I may have felt something for him, but I think it was just a crush.

Jake brought me breakfast in bed, I pushed the thought of Jameson aside and focused on the moment. We sat in bed and watched tv while we had our pancakes and coffee. I looked at Jake and I realize that the person that I've been waiting for might be right in front of me. When I'm with Jake, I almost don't have time to think about my mom and dad, the trauma of falling in love and falling out of love.

"You okay", Jake asked.

"Yeah, I'm just happy", I responded.

I moved closer to Jake, and we cuddled, I felt at ease for a moment. I kept checking my phone to see if Jameson had reached out, but he hasn't. I looked at Jake to ask if we should reach out to Jameson, but this is not the right time for it. I can tell that Jake is also upset by our encounter last night, so I let it go…for now.

NOW: TWO WEEKS TO GO

Jake and I had our final walkthrough with our venue and vendors. We have two weeks to go before our big day! Jake and his groomsmen are planning on going camping for his bachelor weekend. Jake felt bad leaving for the weekend, but he has been very helpful and supportive with wedding plannings that I feel that I could also use a weekend alone to refocus myself and unwind. I haven't had the apartment to myself since we moved in, so, I am kind of looking forward to being alone for a few days. Of course, it's going to feel weird without Jake and it's not that I don't want him around, after everything the last week and a half, I could use some time to myself.

I helped Jake pack his things, I told him my plans for the weekend: deep clean the apartment, order take out, finish writing my vows, and spend the rest of my time in my pajamas while I binge watch Netflix.

"You sure you don't need anything? Here, I'll at least leave some cash so you can tip for your food", Jake said.

"Babe no, I'll be fine I promise! I want you to enjoy your weekend and be with your boys because in two weeks, you will be a married man and I might never let you out of my sight again", I teased.

Jake gave me a kiss, and another, and another. This is his first time leaving me alone for longer than eight hours a day. Ty called Jake to let him know that they are outside, ready to pick him up. I walked Jake to the door and wished him a safe trip. I watched him walk away then I went over to the window to see them drive off. I realized then that it was raining outside, I love when it rains, it's so calming, and it gives me a reason not to leave my house. I settled on the couch, and scrolled through Netflix to find something to watch, then I heard a text come in, I thought that it was Jake, but it was not.

Can we talk? I'm sorry for walking away the other day. Please, let's talk.

It was a text from Jameson, my heart dropped, I froze. How do I respond to this? Two minutes later, another text came through.

Nat, please. I need to talk to you. I just need to talk to you. I'll be at the Riverfront in an hour. I'll be waiting. I just hope that you give me a chance to say what I need to say, then after that, if you don't want to see me or talk to me every again, I'll accept it. Please.

Jameson was pleading to talk to me but what is there to talk about? It's not like we had a past, we have been great friends for years.

Okay.

I finally responded.

SENIOR YEAR

"We're *finally* almost out of here!" Ty expressed.

"I'll drink to that", Jason responded.

It's finals week, then in two weeks, the five of us get to walk across the stage and say goodbye to our college life, and start in the real world, the grown-up world. How scary!

We decided to have a fire at Ty and Jason's to reminisce on our college years just like we did on our very first day of college. Jake and Jameson were grilling food, Ty and Jason were being their silly selves as we listened to Morgan Wallen on the radio with drinks in our hands. I can't believe that most of my high school life, I was so afraid to start college. Yet, here I am, with the people that the old Natalie would have never been friends with. I couldn't help but feel emotional but of course, I can't cry in front of the boys. I decided to soak in this moment and enjoy the last few weeks of being a kid.

"Here, Nat", Jameson handed me a plate with hotdog and chips.

"So, I guess we're all moving to Philadelphia, huh?" Jameson said with a smile on his face.

Jake and I were both hired for our jobs in Philadelphia, then Jameson followed, then Ty, and Jason. It's nice that we'll be in the same city, we might not be able to hangout as often but it's nice to move to a city where we already know other people. I've always been afraid of starting over but I guess it worked out for me this time.

"Hey, hear me out" Ty stood up as if he's about to give a presidential speech.

"Once a month, we do a thing together, whether it's to go out to eat, drinks, or hangout at home. No excuses, we all get together, once a month. That's all, folks", Ty said.

I like this idea, and it seems like everyone did too. We all stood up to toast our drinks, then we spent the rest of the night talking about our early college years. This is great.

I'm looking around to see if I can spot Jade, Alli, and Sam in the crowd. There are so many people in the stadium, it's so hard to see. I got a text from Jade with a picture of where they're sitting, I tried my best to turn around and wave, hopefully I waved at the right people. After sitting for forty minutes, listening to speeches, and special awards, it was finally our turn. I waited patiently for my row to be called, I was feeling nervous, anxious, and happy. I heard Jason and Ty yell my name, I waved hi to Jake, I couldn't find Jameson, but I know that he is here.

It was finally my turn,

Natalie Anderson, Suma Cum Laude

I walked across the stage; I could almost hear Jade's voice as I shook hands with the school president. I made eye contact with Jake and smiled. This is it; I hope that I make my mom proud. But most importantly, I get to start a new chapter with Jake. We found an apartment in Philadelphia and decided to move in together. Our lease starts in two days, so we have to pack our things and head to Philadelphia. Jade was sad that I chose Philadelphia over Colorado, but I did promise her that once a year I will make a trip down to see her and spend the weekend with her. Alli and Sam are both staying in Jersey about two hours from Philadelphia.

It is a privilege and an honor to present to you, Princeton University's class of 2016!

We all cheered and threw our caps in the air. Everyone was jumping and hugging each other, it feels like we all know each other, considering there's hundreds of us graduating today. After we walked out, I stood by the exit to find Jake. We finally found each other, we ran towards each other, Jake lifted me and kissed me. A few moments later Ty and Jason found us, now all we need is Jameson. We saw him walk across the stage; he was sitting towards the back so he may have gone already.

We took pictures, then we finally found Alli, Sam, and Jade.

"Girl!! You did it!", Jade ran towards me and gave me the biggest hug.

I was finally able to introduce Jake, Ty, and Jason to my girls, Jade kept giving me looks of approval behind Jake's back. We decided to head to dinner, Ty and Jason had dinner plans with their families, so they were not able to join us. Jake's parents are meeting us at the restaurant. We texted Jameson the plans for today, but he didn't respond. Jake sent another text to let Jameson know that we are heading out and to join us, but Jameson didn't respond back. Maybe he has plans with his brother and mother.

"Hey Nat, come with me for a minute", Jake said.

"Oh okay, Jade, I'll meet you guys there, we'll be right behind you" I said.

Jake and I were holding hands, constantly being stopped every few steps to say hi and goodbye to the people that we've met over the last four years. Jake was walking fast, I had to tell him to slow down a few times since I was wearing heels. After what seems forever, Jake stopped. He lets my hand go then faced towards me.

"Well? Do you remember?" he asked.

I was confused for a minute then I realized that we're standing under the tree where we had our first lunch during our freshman year, the first time that we met.

"Yeah, it doesn't seem as scary anymore", I said.

Jake puts his right hand in his pocket, he kneels on one knee, then he opened a box with a diamond ring.

"Natalie Anne Anderson, I'm so happy that we met four years ago in this very same spot, and I'm even happier that we get to start a new life together. I promise that I will continue to take care of you, love you, and protect you. Will you do me the honor of being your husband?", Jake looked nervous and happy at the same time.

I froze and felt tears coming down my face. I nodded "yes" and offered him my hand. He stood up and we hugged for a long time. Holy shit! I'm engaged!

I cried tears of joy the whole way to dinner, I can't believe that I am getting married to my best friend! Jake told me that he purchased my ring a while ago, but he was looking for the perfect opportunity to propose. We haven't been together that long, but we have known each other since our freshman year, and I trust that we are making the right decisions for us and our future. This was one of those moments when I wish that I could call my mom and grandma, I wish that they were here to share this day with us.

We made it to dinner, Jade, Alli, Sam, and Jake's family were waiting for us…and Jameson? Jade whispered that he showed up and she heard that his mom had to work right after the ceremony, so Jake's mom insisted that he comes to dinner and celebrate his graduation day too.

"Everyone, if I can please have your attention", Jake announced. Everyone was staring at us as we stood by our seats.

"Nat and I wanted to say our thanks to everyone for being here and celebrating this occasion with us. Umm, well, I don't really know how to say this any other way, but we want to share our engagement with you all", Jake finally said.

Jade, Alli, and Sam all stood up, screamed, and ran to hug me. Jake's parents were ecstatic about this announcement too, Jameson stood up from his seat, with no expression.

"Wait! So, tell us, how did it happen? When??", Jade asked.

"It was right after we split up, Jake took me to the tree where we had our first lunch when we met on our first day, and that's about it", I explained.

Jameson walked over to us, reach out his hand to Jake,

"Congratulations, man", he said to Jake.

Then Jameson gave me a quick hug.

We all proceeded with our dinner, Jake's mom gave a speech about how proud and happy they are for their son and for our engagement. Jameson didn't say much, he said a few words throughout dinner, but he seemed to be okay to sit and listen to the conversations around him. Jake told the story about the ring and when he knew that I was the one then his father congratulated us on our engagement, and we spent the rest of the night drinking and laughing with the people that we love and care for.

After a while I noticed that Jake and Jameson had been standing outside, I could see them through the window. It looks like they're arguing, I don't know what about, but Jake seemed really upset. Jake turned and walked away, leaving Jameson by himself. Jameson then started to walk, lets out a deep sigh as he turned to leave.

"Is everything okay?", I asked Jake.

"Yeah, don't worry about it", he responded then excused himself to use the restroom.

Even though Jake didn't want to say anything, I knew that something was not right. I have noticed that lately, Jake and Jameson have been spending less time together and they always seem tense around each other. Jake always says that it's nothing and that Jameson is having a hard time because of personal family matters. Jameson has stopped talking to me, occasionally, he'll respond to my texts or will join us for lunch or dinner, but he only talks to me as if we barely know each other.

"I'll be right back", I said to Jake.

I ran outside to try and catch Jameson by the time I made it out he was already halfway down the street.

"Jameson!", I called for him, but he didn't stop as if he couldn't hear me.

"Jameson! Wait!", I continued to run after him.

He finally stopped; I was out of breath by the time I caught up to him.

"Oh my God you walk so fast, I've been yelling for you", I said while I try to catch my breath.

"Sorry, I didn't hear you", he said, I knew he was lying.

"What's wrong? Why didn't you say goodbye?", I asked.

"You seemed busy, so I didn't want to interrupt", he said.

"I saw you and Jake talking but it looked like you guys were arguing. I asked Jake what was wrong, but he wouldn't say. So, what's up? Are you okay?", I asked again.

"Yeah, we're fine, don't worry about it", he responded.

"No, I'm tired of you and Jake telling me not to worry about something when clearly, I should be worried and clearly it has something to do with me. Please, tell me, what is it that you guys have been fighting about?", I protested.

Jameson turned to look at me, his eyes were full of pain and sadness. He tried to avoid my eyes, I stared into his eyes while I patiently wait for him to give me an answer.

"I'm happy for you, Nat. I don't know, I guess I'm just jealous that Jake has his life in order better than I do. Please go back to him and enjoy the rest of your evening. Don't worry about me, I'll talk to you later", he said then turned to walk away.

I stood there feeling defeated. I know that he's not telling me the whole truth, I know that there's something that he wants to say. I stood there hoping that he would turn around and open up, but he kept on walking. So, I turned around and started to head back towards the restaurant.

It does upset me to see us drift apart especially Jake and Jameson. I wish that they would tell me if there were an issue between them but neither one of them seems to want to talk, maybe this is just how guys deal with issues? Who knows, but it would be great if I could find out. We had another quiet drive home; Jake didn't say much, and I could tell that he is still upset about whatever it was that they were arguing about. He did apologize for ruining our engagement night which I told him that it was fine and that today is still a very special day. Jake smiled and was quiet the rest of our drive.

NOW: TWO WEEKS TO GO

I held onto my phone as I debated whether I should meet Jameson or not. I know what he's going to say, I know that it won't do anything but upset me. Will I be doing Jake wrong if I meet with our friend who confessed that he's had feelings for me this whole time? Will it be wrong to go behind Jake's back knowing that our wedding is two weeks away? I asked myself whether I should text or call Jake, I don't want to ruin his trip or his friendship with Jameson, but I do plan on telling him about this when the timing is right.

I grabbed by purse and my keys as I headed downstairs, once I made it to my car, I sat in silence. I looked at my phone to see if Jameson had sent me another text, but he didn't. I decided to finally start my car and gathered the courage to go. I don't know what's going to happen and I hate this feeling. My chest hurts and I can feel myself wanting to cry but I decided to fight through my emotions. I'm angry at Jameson, there's no doubt about that, but I am even more angry that I feel that after today, I will lose one of the most important people in my life. And that I think is what will hurt the most.

I pulled into the parking lot, I decided to park by the river, I took a deep breath and waited for Jameson to show up. I watched for Jameson's car to pull in, I started to tear up when I saw his car. Jameson parked a few spots down from mine, he kept his head down after he turned his car off, I unlocked my doors assuming that he will eventually come to me.

I watched Jameson walk towards me as I listen to the sound of the rain hitting the roof of my car. Every step he took made my stomach turn; I knew what this was about when he asked to meet up. I watched as he took his right hand out of his pocket to open the car door, he sat in the passenger seat, let out a big sigh, and finally he took his red hood off his head. We sat in silence for a minute before he finally opened his mouth to speak but he hesitated and closed them right back.

In my head I thought, "dear Lord please just say something". But I sat there quietly with my head down just like his. We listened to the sound of the rain and the static coming from the radio. I wanted to tell him that I know, I've known for so long and if it makes him feel any better, it hurts me just as much. I could hear him breathing heavily, I know he's trying to gather the courage to say it out loud.

"I need to confess something...to tell you something" he finally said, quietly while keeping his head down. His hands were fidgeting with his car keys, and I could tell from his tone how scared and nervous he must feel. But I let it go, and I let him go at his own pace.

"You have no idea how awful I feel about this and saying it out loud makes me feel dumber, but I need to tell you." He cleared his throat as he finally lifted his head, but he wasn't looking at me.

He was watching the windshield wiper as it continues to wipe off every drop of rain even though it's pointless because the rain doesn't seem like it will let up anytime soon. I guess that's how we both feel inside too. We both know that no matter what we're about to say is just as pointless.

"I've been...I've been in love with you. It wasn't something that happened overnight but the more I got to know you, the more I felt strongly about you." He paused.

"I know it's wrong and I don't expect anything to come out of this, but I need to tell you. I'm sorry that my timing is wrong. But I can't watch you walk down that aisle in two weeks without telling you how I've felt. It's selfish, I know, but I had to tell you." He shook his head; I looked over to see that his eyes were turning red, and tears were starting to build up.

I took a few breaths before saying anything back. I knew how he felt but I didn't think that I was right. I know that he's waiting for me to say something, perhaps he thinks I might get angry and call him selfish, which he is, and I can't believe that this is happening now. But I gathered the courage to look at him and say,

"I know...I've known for a while", I said quietly.

The look on his face will forever be engraved in my head. He wasn't surprised that I knew, he looked apologetic.

"I knew but I didn't say anything… I didn't know what to say. But I know, it was no secret." I said to him.

He turned his head towards me and looked me directly in the eyes, when he said, "I love you.".

Hearing those words come out of his mouth instantly made me cry my eyes out. He was quiet for a while as he watched me cry. I couldn't get myself to stop crying, I tried to collect myself, but it was becoming harder and harder every second that I know he's sitting right next to me. All I can think of is how awful this will make Jake feel if he finds out that his own best friend has strong feelings for his soon-to-be wife. I was finally able to calm myself down and attempted to look back at him, but I couldn't.

"I know", I said, finally.

"I've always known how you felt about me. I remember our freshman year and how upset you were at the picnic when Jake offered me his sweatshirt. Then the night when I thought you'd kiss me. Then I thought I knew for sure the night that you found out about me and Jake. But then, you acted like everything was fine, you didn't say anything then so why are you telling me this now?", I said.

Jameson kept his head down and kept quiet.

"Damn it Jameson! Answer me! You said you wanted to talk so talk!", I demanded.

"I'm sorry", he said.

That's it?! "I'm sorry"?!

"You can't just say you love me then say you're sorry! Oh my, Jameson! Why did you wait this long?! How am I supposed to walk down the aisle in two weeks?? You're Jake's *best man* so why are you doing this now??", I finally let out.

"I don't know", he said.

"I…I don't know I thought that…I don't know", his voice started to fade.

"What were you expecting? What were you expecting that would come out after this? You told me you love me, you had six years Jameson, six years to tell me so why did you wait until now? Are you expecting me to leave him at the altar? What kind of a friend, no wait, what kind of a brother are you?!", I said as I turned to finally look at him directly in the eyes.

We looked at each other in the eyes both with tears flowing down our faces. I looked at him with anger, yet I felt sorry for him. His eyes say they're sorry and I know that we both wish that we were never in this position to begin with.

"I'm sorry. I don't know why I waited this long. But the thought of you walking down the aisle and saying your vows and seeing you with him for the rest of our lives, I thought I could live with that idea Nat. I really did. For a while I thought that I was over you then every time I see you," he grabs my hands and held them against his chest.

"But every time I see you…every time I see you smile, listen to your voice, listen to your laugh…it pulls me right back in. Every time I close my eyes, I see you walking into the lecture hall and seeing you for the very first time. The first time you talked to me, that entire walk to our next class together, and everything after that. It's like I can't get you out of my head", he said as he continued to hold my hands.

I sat there in silence; I'm trying to wake myself up because clearly this is just a dream…right? He didn't really say those things, we're friends, *just* friends. Jameson started to lean closer to me, I looked up and our eyes meet. I can feel his breath as he pulled me closer to him.

"Jameson", I whispered.

"No", I pulled back.

"We can't, I'm…I'm sorry if you thought that anything will happen between us. Whatever happened in the past, everything that happened then it's all in the past. I am going to marry Jake in two weeks. I love him. I love you because you have been a very important part of my life. But we can't do this, not now, not ever", I said apologetically and continued to pull my hands away from his.

He leaned back and lets out a big sigh. He puts his hands over his face then he quickly grabbed my face and kissed me.

What the hell?! I tried to pull back and tell him no, but I couldn't get the words out. He stopped for a moment and our eyes meet again then slowly he went for another kiss and this time I let him. His lips touching mine and his hands on my face I knew I was defeated. I knew it needed to stop but I kissed him back. Every memory from the very first day that we met started coming back to me. Slowly, we pulled away from each other.

"You need to leave. Please. Go.", I said quietly and turned my head the other way.

I heard him open the door, but I didn't turn to look at him, I waited until I hear him close the door, I turned my head and watched him walk away. I laid my head back as I bawled my eyes out. All I can think of is how dishonest and how I've betrayed Jake. Of all people, I betrayed my best friend and for what? For someone who didn't have the guts to tell me how he felt about me until now? What am I going to do? How am I going to tell any of this to Jake two weeks before our wedding?

I tossed my keys on the kitchen counter, kicked my shoes off and went straight for the couch. All I can do is bury my head in a pillow and cry. I hear my phone vibrate and saw a text from Jake,

I miss you! I can't wait to come home.

I set my phone to the side, how am I supposed to respond to my fiancé after what just happened. I laid on my back with my eyes closed. I felt helpless, I didn't have an ounce of energy to get up or even look at my phone. All I can see is Jameson, the way he was close to my face, the way his lips felt when they touched mine. Then I see Jake and how he doesn't deserve someone like me. Jameson and I, we don't deserve Jake. We betrayed him.

ONE MORE WEEK: CONFESSION

Since Jake came home from his bachelor trip, it's been getting harder and harder to avoid telling him what had happened on the first night that he was away. Jake told me that Jameson showed up at the cabin already drunk. He said that Jameson was mumbling and could barely stand when he got out of the car. The guys were not so sure how he managed to drive up the mountains in his condition. After he told me what happened with Jameson, I have been avoiding having a conversation especially when Jameson's name is involved. Jake had asked if I was okay on multiple occasions, but I told him that it's just stress from the last-minute wedding planning.

I told Jake that I need to run some errands, not really, but I needed to get out of the apartment, away from all the wedding stuff, and away from Jake. Not because I don't want to marry him but the more I'm around him, the more I am reminded of what I did behind his back. Jake told me to take my time and that he'll take care of making dinner. I grabbed my purse and headed for the door. I decided to walk instead of taking my car. I kept walking until I reached the coffee shop where Jameson first told me how he felt about me. I looked at the table through the window where we sat and where everything fell apart. I have lost one of my friends, someone that I considered family. I've decided to delete the text messages between Jameson and me. I wasn't trying to hide anything from Jake, but I didn't want him to find those texts before I can tell him myself.

I stopped at the flower shop to drop off the final payment for our wedding. I received a text from our bridesmaids group chat, Jade sent a picture of my wedding dress, she's in charge of keeping my dress safe until the big day. All the girls are ecstatic about the big day, and I am too but I feel that I can't walk down the aisle and start a new journey with Jake with a secret. The sun was starting to set so I started to walk back home, I keep thinking of when and how I should tell Jake what happened and why I didn't try to stop it. I mean I did but there wasn't much I could do. Or I can just not tell him and live miserably for the rest of our lives.

I opened the door and found Jake in the dining area waiting for me. He made pasta and chicken, he had candles lit, and wine on the table. I started to tear up then he slowly came over to me, he takes my purse, and led me to the table. He pulls my chair out and waited to sit me like he's a server in a five-star restaurant. Then he poured some wine in my glass before he sat down across from me. I was too stunned to speak.

"I know that you've worked so hard to make sure that our day is perfect, and I know that you've been in a lot of pressure this past year, so I made your favorite as a thank you. And that I want you to know that for the rest of our lives, I will always have your back. Maybe not always with chicken and pasta, but you know what I mean", he said as he grabbed me for a hug and kissed me.

I couldn't help but start to cry, what have I done? I don't deserve this man, this perfect and the most supportive man that I have ever met.

"Jake…" I said as I wiped the tears off my face.

"I need to tell you something and I should have told you right away, but I didn't", I finally said.

I looked up at Jake, he didn't look surprised or bothered at all, he looked calm.

"I…when you…when you left…I and…", I couldn't get the words out.

"You and Jameson?", he finally said.

I was shocked when he mentioned Jameson's name, he knows?! How?? Ugh, I bet that Jameson told him while they were away.

"I figured it was something to do with Jameson", he said.

"Did I ever told you the conversation that I had with him the night that we got engaged?", Jake asked. I shook my head, "no", and didn't say a word.

"I don't know if you remember but at one point Jameson walked out all upset so I followed him. When I went to check on him, he told me that I was the worst friend for proposing to you. Then he told me that he's had feelings for you since our freshman year. I told him that I didn't know because he never talked to you in any way that would have hinted how he felt for you. But I guess that night after a few drinks, he finally let it all spill, so he told me. But I knew that at the time you didn't know", he paused.

"I've known all along. The night at the frat formal when he got drunk because he was so upset when we finally told everyone that we started dating. I've known since the last semester of our freshman year. He told me that he was falling for you, but he didn't want to ruin anything with you, so he wanted to wait for the perfect time. Then he disappeared that summer and we spent a lot of time alone without him and that was when I started to fall for you", Jake said.

The more Jake talked about how he's known this whole-time kind of rubbed me the wrong way. I mean, did he ask me out just so Jameson wouldn't?

"I didn't ask you out because of him, please, don't get me wrong. That summer he was so distant, and it felt that I've lost my brother. It was you who I was able to turn to and talk to when I needed someone. That's why I fell in love with you, Nat", Jake's voice started to fade as if he's guilty for not telling me any of these.

"Then last weekend, Jameson showed up, again, drunk. I helped him up to his room, we put him in bed then I heard him say your name. Then he kept saying how sorry he was, he was apologizing to you", Jake paused for a minute.

"I was about to walk out when he said he loved you and that he would kiss you again if he could", I looked up and Jake was staring right at me. He looked broken and angry. I've never seen this look on his face before.

"Jake…" I tried to tell him what happened.

"So, the next day I decided to just confront him. I told him what he said while he was drunk. He told me that you met with him after I left and that he *confessed* to you and how you tried pushing him away, but he wouldn't let you. I punched him. I've never punched or hit anyone let alone my best friend, my own brother", Jake was about to get up when I asked him to hear me out.

"Jake, I know I shouldn't have but part of me wanted to hear him out because he's important to me too and I didn't want our wedding to be the last time that I see him. He was my friend and someone that I trusted for years. Jake, please believe me when I say that I didn't know that he was going to say all that and that he was going to…kiss me", I finally confessed.

"I didn't put any of it together until recently. The last game night that we had he told me that he found someone in college, but he was too late. Then a few days after while I was at the coffee shop downtown, I saw him then he walked over to me. Then he told me that I knew who the girl was, the more he talked that was when I realized that he was talking about me. I remember some things from college, but I didn't realize then and I certainly did not know until he told me", I looked at Jake, hoping that we can move pass this.

"Jake, I know that I was wrong. I should have never met with him after you left, I thought about calling you first to tell you but I…"

"Oh wow, so you thought about asking if I'd be okay if you met up with my best friend not too long after I left?", Jake angrily interrupted me.

"What? No! Of course not, I just…I wanted to tell you that I knew about how he felt. But I…I'm sorry, Jake", I stood up and slowly walked towards Jake, but he pulls back.

"Please, just let me explain the whole thing, I was wrong. I should have never gone behind your back. I should have told him no, I shouldn't have given him the closure that he wanted, I shouldn't have answered his call, I should have stayed home where I was supposed to wait for you all weekend until you came home. I'm sorry! I'm so sorry", I started to panic and cry.

Jake slowly takes a few steps towards me and pulls me close to his chest to try and comfort me. Even when I'm in the wrong how can he set his emotions aside to comfort me.

"He told me that he loved me", I said quietly.

Jake and I slowly let each other go, I looked up, our eyes meet.

"So, what now?", he said.

"What do you mean?", I asked.

"We have exactly seven days, what do you want to do?", he asked.

We stared at each other, in silence, my heart sinks. What now?

THREE MORE DAYS

The last four days has been rough, Jake and I barely talked to each other since Saturday night. He has been sleeping on the pull-out couch, but he tucks me to bed and kisses me in the forehead. Every meal we've had has been shared in silence, some nights if we're lucky maybe a few words here and there. Jake doesn't seem angry but he's shutdown and I've been on my tiptoes around him. I try talking to him about the wedding, all he said was he was going to pick up his tux on Thursday and "hope that it fits".

I tried asking if he wanted to shop for clothes together for our rehearsal dinner on Friday, but he said that he'll find something in his closet, but he'll come with if I want him to. I can't help but worry that he's going to call off our wedding or that he'll leave me at the altar. I told him that Jade offered to take me shopping for our rehearsal dinner clothes. He said, "cool", then got up from the couch and walked away.

Jade and I met downtown and headed for the boutique. She was going on and on about how I'm going to be a wife in 73 hours and how excited she is to see me in my dress. When we finally made it to the store, Jade kept immediately handed me a handful of dresses to try on. None of it looked right, then Jade found a simple yet elegant white cocktail dress and told me to try it then we can leave.

"Oh my god, Nat! That's it! Look at you!", Jade got up to get a closer look of me in my dress.

I started crying and was about to head back into the dressing room when Jade grabbed my arm.

"Hey, what's going on? You've been so quiet? Oh honey, it's perfectly normal to feel anxious and nervous!" Jade gives me a hug then I pulled away slowly.

"It's not that…Jade, I screwed up. I don't think Jake is going to want to marry me anymore", I cried.

"What?? What happened? Nat, you know how crazy in love he is with you! He would never call the wedding off", Jade tried to reassure me.

"I messed up. I…I kissed another guy", I said quietly.

Jade then grabs my arm and led me to the dressing room; she shuts the door behind her.

"What?! Who?? When?? Natalie what the hell is going on?", Jade was full of questions, rightfully so.

"Jameson happened. The day that Jake left for his bachelor trip, Jameson texted me and said that he wanted to talk. Then one thing led to another, he confessed that he's been in love with me then he kissed me. Jade, I tried to stop him, you have to believe me. But…"

"But what? What, Nat?", she asked.

"At first, I tried pushing him away then he went in for another kiss and that's when I let him. I kissed him back", I confessed.

Jade was quiet, she puts her hands on her head while pacing back and forth.

"And you told Jake?", she asked.

"No, Jameson did. Jake said that Jameson showed up drunk that evening then he mumbled some things in his sleep, something about how he loves me. Then the next day Jake confronted him and that's when he told Jake how he felt about me including the kiss", I responded.

"Oh my god! Nat, you know that I love you and I will always have your back but not this time, not with this. Jake doesn't deserve that", she scolded me.

"I know…I know! Damn it!" I took the dresses and threw them on the floor.

I sat on the chair and put my hands over my face as I cried.

"I know. I messed up, I ruined it Jade, I'm going to lose him", I cried.

"What if he calls off the wedding? What if he doesn't show up? What was I thinking??", I started to panic.

Jade grabs me to comfort me and I know that she's angry with me. I couldn't bring myself to tell her the whole story, I was too ashamed to face the fact that I may have ruined my own marriage.

"Here, get changed. I'll take your dress upfront", she said quietly as she walked out.

I stayed in the room for a while and tried pull myself together. I walked out of the dressing room, and I knew that half of these women were listening to our conversation. They're all probably thinking what a shitty person I am.

Jade and I were supposed to get dinner afterwards, but we decided to call off the night and go home. She drops me off, we didn't say a word the whole ride home.

"Hey Nat, it's going to be okay. Just let him cool off", Jade said.

I offered a half smile as I turned to get out of the car. I took a deep breath before heading into our apartment. I slowly opened the door, the lights were turned off, but I could hear the TV in the living room. Jake was watching TV in the dark, I noticed a few empty bottles of beer sitting on the coffee table. Jake looks over to my direction, looks away, then takes a sip of his beer.

"I got my dress for the dinner", I said.

Jake didn't say anything, he nods his head in acknowledgement. I debated whether I should walk over to him and try to talk but he didn't seem ready, so I started to walk towards our room.

"I talked to Jameson today", he said.

I was shocked to hear that they talked, as far as I know Jameson was dead to him.

"He had to return his tux, they gave him the wrong size", Jake said.

"Oh, okay". I said as I turned to walk away.

"He asked about you", Jake said almost in a condescending way.

"Jake, we don't have to talk if you're not ready", I responded.

"I just thought I should tell you that he asked about you", he said.

"Okay, cool. Is there anything else?", I said but this time I was feeling irritable.

"I figured you should know, that's all", he said as he took another sip of his drink.

I scuffed and shook my head then started to walk down the hall.

"Yup, guess he's going to stand by my side and watch me marry the woman that he loves", he said under his breath but loud enough that I could hear him.

I dropped my bags on the floor and stormed to the living room.

"I get it, okay?! You don't need to be so harsh, I told you what happened and I'm sorry that it happened, but it did. So, tell me, is this how it's going to be forever?", I finally snapped.

"Forever? I didn't think there was a, "*forever*", you know since you and my best friend made out", Jake said as he stood up from the couch.

"I can't do this, enjoy the rest of your night", I said as I headed towards the door.

"Where the hell are you going?!", he yelled.

"I need some air", I responded as I slammed the door shut behind me.

Jake and I have never yelled at each other before, sure, we've argued but we've never fought. I realized that I forgot my car keys, but I didn't want to go back so I walked and eventually found myself at the bar a couple blocks from our apartment. I walked in, the place was packed which surprised me because it's a Wednesday night but what do I know? I never go out on my own, let alone on a weeknight. I grabbed a seat at the bar and ordered a drink. I'm pretty sure everyone was looking at me, I mean I'm not dressed for a night out and not to mention I've been bawling my eyes out.

After two drinks, I saw someone from the corner of my eyes take the seat next to me. All I saw was their arms then I finally looked up. Oh, for heaven's sake! Can't I just have some time to myself?! Of all people it had to be Jameson.

I looked at him and rolled my eyes. I started to get the bartenders attention to pay for my drinks.

"I got it", Jameson said as he pushed my hand and card away.

I shook my head and grabbed my purse then headed for the door. I started to walk as fast as I could hoping that Jameson will take a while to pay for the drinks and by the time he makes it out, I'll be long gone.

"Nat!", I heard Jameson call my name.

Oh, great, he made it out just in time. Lovely.

Jameson ran after me; he taps my shoulder and cuts me off.

"Hey, are you okay?", he asked.

"What?", I responded.

"You're by yourself and you never drink during the week, what's going on?", he asked, he sounded genuinely concerned.

"What's going on? Oh, Jameson, I don't know. Maybe it has something to do with my best friend making a confession about how he loves me, *two weeks* before my wedding. Maybe it has something to do with kissing my fiancé's best friend. Oh, and to complete the whole package, my fiancé found out about all of it from his drunken best friend on his own bachelor trip! So, everything has been *great*, Jameson.", I snapped.

"Okay, hey, I'm sorry", he tried to stop me again from walking away.

"You're sorry? For which part?", I responded sarcastically.

"For all of it, I should have never put you in this position. How's Jake? Do you want me to talk to him?", he asked.

"Yes, Jameson because the last person that he needs to talk to is the person who caused all of this!", I yelled at him.

"You still have a bruise on your face, and you think that you can fix all of this? My fiancé has been sleeping on the couch since he got back, and I don't even know if we're still getting married! And it's all thanks to you, so no, you've done enough", I said loudly, I'm pretty sure the people across the street can hear our entire conversation.

"Let me at least walk you home, it's late and you're by yourself. Or at least let me get you an Uber", he offered.

"The last thing that I need right now is any help from you, so please, just leave me alone", I pushed Jameson out of the way as I walked away as fast as I could.

At some point, I turned to see if he was still following me, he was. I finally made it to my apartment complex.

"I don't hate you. I hate the situation that we're in, I hate that I hurt Jake", I said to Jameson over my shoulders.

I turned around, he was standing away from me. I needed him to know that I don't hate him, I'm angry at him, at myself, but I could never hate him.

"I'm sorry that I put you in this position. I never meant to hurt you or Jake. It was stupid on my end, I'm sorry", Jameson responded as he slowly turned and walked away.

I slowly unlocked the door and closed it behind me. I quietly put my purse on the counter and found that Jake was still awake, still in the same spot where I left, but with a few more empty bottles in front of him.

We stared at each other; Jake was sitting on the couch, the light from the TV was only source of light that we had. But I could tell that he had been crying even though I can't really see his face. I opened my mouth to say anything, but I decided not to. I kept my head down and slowly walked back to our room. I closed the door behind me, sat on the floor, and broke down. I heard Jake get up from the couch and I could hear his footsteps getting closer, but I didn't move. I could hear him standing on the other side of the door. I didn't know what to do, I didn't know what would happen if I stood up and opened the door, will he welcome me back with open arms? Or will he tell me to pack up and call everything off?

THE REHEARSAL DINNER

I opened my eyes and looked to my left; Jake must have spent the night in the living room again. I rubbed my eyes and reached for my phone, I have a bunch of text messages from our bridesmaids group chat, messages from Jake's mom, and a lot of last-minute questions from the vendors. I should be excited about today; I get to finally see our venue and all the hard work that I have put in the last two years. I should be excited that this means we only have 24-hours until we say our, "I do's". I should be excited that tomorrow I finally get to wear my wedding dress and marry Jake. But I feel nothing but sadness, that's all. I'm just…sad.

I tried to gather the courage to get out of bed, I heard Jake walking around in the kitchen so I figured that I should too. I had a different scenario in my head about the last 24-hours before our wedding day. Jake and I would wake up next to each other, we'll stay in bed for a bit and take it all in, we'd make breakfast together and talk about how we got here. You know, the picture-perfect couple thing. We would get ready together for the rehearsal dinner, Jake would try to mess with me while I do my hair and makeup, then I'd pretend to be angry at him, then he'd grab me, kiss me, and tell me that he can't wait to marry me.

I sighed before opening our bedroom door, I slowly made it out to the kitchen. I found Jake sitting in the living room with what I'm assuming is an Irish coffee. He didn't bother to look up or acknowledgement me, he kept his eyes on his phone. I stood there waiting to see if he'll say anything, I thought of saying hi or good morning, but he didn't, and I couldn't find the courage to say anything to him either. I slowly walked away to make coffee and toast.

"What time do you need me to be there?", Jake asked.

I turned and he was standing on the other side of the counter, as he makes his best attempt to not look at me in the eyes.

"I figured we could drive together, it would be weird if we drove separate to our own rehearsal dinner", I responded.

"Yeah...guess just let me know when you're ready to leave then", he said quietly.

Jake turned to walk back to the living room.

"Jake", I called.

He turns towards me, but his eyes laid on the counter.

"Can we talk?", I said.

"About what?", he said as he shook his head.

"You know about what...we're getting married in 24hrs, I just don't know if this is something that you still want", I finally said.

Jake didn't say anything, he took a deep breath and paused for a minute.

"Why? You don't want to get married anymore?", he finally responded.

"I mean I do", I took a step towards him, but he took a step back.

"I want to marry you and I want to grow old with you. I know that this is all my fault and I screwed up what we had. But you can't even look at me or even acknowledge when I'm around", I said.

"You're right, Nat", he said as he rubbed his face.

"I don't know anymore, I used to be able to look at you and know that I'm with the person I can trust. My best friend. But what you and Jameson did, I know it wasn't all your fault that he fell for you but the fact that you saw him behind my back, and I had to find out from him that you kissed each other. I don't know if I can trust you anymore, if I'm being honest", Jake responded.

I put my head down and tears started to run down my face. I mean he's right. What kind of a marriage are we going to have if he can't trust me. His feelings are valid, and I wouldn't blame him if he didn't show tomorrow.

"I know", I said quietly.

"I screwed up. I shouldn't have agreed to meet him behind your back. But Jake you have to believe me. I love you and only you. I know that my actions say otherwise, and I know I need to earn your trust back. Please believe me when I say that I do want to spend the rest of our lives together.", I pleaded.

I walked closer to Jake; he took another step back.

"So, now what?", I asked.

Jake sighed and rubbed his head. He finally looked up then our eyes met.

"Can we make it work?", he asked.

I opened my mouth to respond as I continue to cry in front of him. He looks very hurt and unsure.

"I do. I want to but only if you'll let me make it up to you", I responded.

"Nat, it's not about you making it up to me. Can I trust you? Can I trust that you wouldn't let another man kiss you?", he asked.

"I do…you *can* trust me. I promise that I'll spend the rest of our lives making it up to you. It was a mistake, and I don't intend for something like that to happen ever again", I responded as I moved closer to Jake.

We're two feet apart, Jake moved closer. Jake took his hand to wipe the tears off my face. Then he slowly put his other hand on my shoulder and slowly rubbed my shoulders. He took a deep breath and pulled me to his chest. I continued to cry, I felt him kiss the top of my head and hugged me as tight as he could. I missed this, the way he smells, the way his hands felt, the way he kisses me. This is the man I want to spend forever with.

Jake slowly pulled away, he grabs my face and leaned in for a kiss. Our first kiss since the chaos started three weeks ago. He took my hands and led me to our bedroom; this is the first time he's stepping foot in our own room. Slowly, he lays me down, I kept my eyes shut. If this is a dream I don't want to wake up. I felt his hands on every inch of my body. Before I knew it, we were naked and we're as close as we can be to each other. This is the man I'm going to marry, the only man that I ever want to kiss me, touch me, hug me.

We arrived at the venue for our rehearsal dinner. Jake wore a navy-blue button up shirt, black pants, and his brown shoes. I looked down and noticed that he is wearing the silver watch that I got him the month after we moved into our apartment. I wore a simple white cocktail dress, silver heels, and decided to put my hair in a low updo. Jake came around to open my door, he grabs my hand, and we walked in together.

Everyone from the wedding party is here, his parents, and my aunt Jean were talking around the corner. Jade made eye contact with me and gave me a smile.

"There's our bride", Jade said and hugged me tight.

Jake lets my hand go and continued to greet everyone.

"I'll be right back", he said as he gave me a kiss on my cheek.

I watched Jake walk towards Jameson who was standing by the exit. They stood next to each other with their hands in their pockets. Just as Jake seemed that he was about to say something, Jake's mother came up to me.

"Hi honey", says Jeanine.

"Hi Jeanine", I responded as we gave each other a hug.

"So, how's our boy doing? How are you doing?", she asked.

"We're good, we're excited. Although I can't believe that we're getting married tomorrow", I said.

"Did I ever told you the time when Jake was in 2nd grade?" she asked.

I shook my head, "no".

"He came home from school and went straight to our bedroom. When I asked him what he was doing, he said that he wanted one of his father's fancy suits. Of course, I asked him what he needs a suit for. Then Jake said that he was getting married because he made a new friend that day. I laughed then I asked him if he knew what marriage means. He responded, "it's when two people want to grow old together". I'm glad that he found you, that he finally gets to wear his own fancy suit and be a husband", Jeanine said.

"That's cute. I promise you that I will take great care of him. We'll start a family eventually and go through life together", I said.

"I know. Whatever happens don't ever stop loving each other. Don't go to bed angry, always remember that communication is the key to all relationships", Jeanine said as she gave me a kiss on the cheek and walked away.

"If everyone is here then I suppose we can get started!", said Irene the event coordinator.

Irene directed everyone where to go, the order for the procession, everyone's que to stand up when it's my turn to walk down the aisle. Jake and his groomsmen walked down first, then the bridesmaids, our ring bearer and flower girl. Then it was my turn. As my as it pains me that my mom and grandmother are not here to walk me down the aisle, I know that they're watching over me. Jake asked me multiple times if I was sure about not inviting my father, but I told him that he has missed out so many years of my life that this is no different. Plus, it didn't feel right for him to give me away.

I stood at the end of the aisle and locked eyes with Jake, but I couldn't help but notice Jameson who is standing next to him with his head down. I started to take a few steps forward and felt my heart beating out of my chest even though this is only a rehearsal.

ONE SUMMER LATER

My freshman year turned out to be the best time of my life! It almost made me sad to pack my things and move back home for a few months. I couldn't wait to go back for next semester. Since my father lived six hours ago, Jade and her parents has offered for me to stay with them over breaks. Jade's mom setup the guest bedroom to be my room. Jade and I have always talked about living together once we are older, but we ended up going to different schools so that never happened but maybe after we graduate Jade will decide to move back home.

Jake and Jameson helped me pack my stuff and load my car. They live 20 minutes from each other back home which is only an hour and a half from Jade's parents. Before leaving for summer, the three of us talked about hanging out over break and to stay in touch so we don't lose contact with each other. Jameson said that he'll be working most days over break but he's going to try his best to come visit. Jake said that he'll check-in on me whenever he gets the chance to. I'm glad that I met both, they made my first year memorable.

As soon as I pulled into Jade's driveway, she came running out the front door with her arms open wide.

"Natty!!!! You're finally home!", she yelled as she attacked me with hugs.

We squeezed each other as tight as we could. Jade's dad came to help me unload my car, Jade's mom welcomed me with open arms, ugh, it feels so good to be home. Jade was talking my ears off the moment I arrived, her dog Olivia came running to greet me. I followed Jade's mom upstairs to the guest room where I'll be staying this summer.

"I'll let you get settled honey, it's so great to have you home", said Janette, Jade's mom.

Jade stood by the doorway then slowly closed the door behind her.

"So...tell me EVERYTHING. How are things with Jameson and Jake??" she pried.

"There's nothing to tell Jade, they're both my best friends", I responded.

"You're blushing! Come on, Nat, we haven't seen each other in months, I want all the details", Jade begged.

I took my suitcase and started to unpack; I walked over to the dressed to put my shirts away when I finally decided to share the last few weeks with Jake.

"Well, if you must know, I think there might be something going on with Jake", I said.

Jade propped herself on the bed with a huge smile on her face.

"But I don't know, I don't want to ruin my friendship with him. I might just be overthinking things", I said.

"Details Nat, details!", Jade teased.

"Ugh...fine. The last two months of school we have been spending a lot of time with each other. And...he kind of said something before I left school", I paused.

"He said that he doesn't know what he'd do this summer without seeing me so he wants to hangout when we can", I said.

"Omg! Nat! So, how do you feel about him?", Jade asked.

"I mean, he is good looking. He's kind, sweet, funny, and he gets my little quirks. If he asked me out maybe I'll say yes", I responded.

"Girls! Come down for snacks when you're ready!", Jade's mom called.

"Coming!", Jade responded.

"We are not done with this conversation", Jade teased as she headed out the door.

I finished unpacking my clothes when I received a text from Jake,

Made it home, how are things with Jade and her family? I'm bored already.

I smiled but I decided not to respond just yet.

Jade and I got a part-time job for the summer at the local café. It makes things easier this way, we can carpool, and nothing beats working with your best friend.

"Hey, Nat! Can you come help the customer out there? I have to take this stuff back", said Jade.

I walked out to the front counter,

"Good morning, how can I help…", I paused.

"Jameson!", I yelled as I ran around the counter to give him a hug.

"What are you doing here?!", I said.

"I have the day off, so I figured I'd come out and visit. Are you allowed to take a break?", he asked.

"She's good, go take your break Nat", Jade responded as she walked past me and Jameson with a "gotcha" look on her face.

I was too stunned to speak, we walked out to the tables up front to catch up.

"So, how's your summer going so far? How's life at, The Good Morning café?", Jameson asked.

"It's going okay, I guess. I just needed something to keep me busy and make money this summer. But, how about you? How's your summer and how are things with your mom?", I responded.

"It's okay, I guess. Mom works overnight shifts at the hospital so I'm usually home with Zach", he said.

I took a bite of my donut, Jameson reached over to wipe the icing off my face. We stared into each other's eyes, he smiled, I was embarrassed that I still like a child.

Jameson cleared his throat and asked if I had anything planned after work. I told him no and offered to show him around if he'll be around for a while. Jameson agreed. He said that he'll walk around the shopping area while I finish at work which should be over in three hours. I walked back inside the café to find Jade standing at the counter with a smile on her face.

"You know your neck might break if you keep tilting your head that way", I said in a joking and sarcastic way to Jade.

"So…*that's* Jameson. He's hot", Jade said in a prying way.

"Yes, that is my *friend* Jameson", I said.

"Your *friend* who drove almost an hour and a half at nine in the morning to surprise you. Yeah, he's your friend", she said.

"Jade…he's just a friend, he said he has the day off so that's why he's here. Nothing more", I said.

"Natalie Anne Anderson, I think you and I both know that a guy won't get up at seven in the morning on their day off and drive sixty miles just to get coffee", Jade said.

"I will be home later, I'm taking him sightseeing after work", I said.

"Sightseeing? In Woodbridge?", Jade asked.

I looked at her, smiled, and gave her a kiss on her forehead as I ignore the rest of her prying.

Jameson was standing outside the shop, he's wearing a white t-shirt, jeans, and his brown hair was slicked back. His hands are in his pockets as he waited patiently for me to come out. I took a deep breath, I took my hair out of my ponytail, there's not much I can do. I'm wearing my work uniform.

"Hey", I said.

Jameson turned to look at me with a soft smile on his face.

"So, I'm ready for my tour of Woodbridge, where to?", he asked.

I smiled and we walked down the sidewalk together. Jameson talked about his summer job and how he can't believe that his younger brother is going into the eighth grade this school year. We were about to cross the street when Jameson grabbed my waist and pulled me back.

"What a jackass! Are you okay?", Jameson asked.

I was stunned and obviously very oblivious to my surroundings that I didn't realize I was about to get hit by a car.

"That's Jersey drivers for you, thanks", I responded.

Something about his hands on my waist and being pressed against him for half a second made my heartbeat too fast. Jameson puts his right hand on my back to guide me as if he's afraid that I'll end up getting hurt. We finally made it to a park where there's food trucks and lots of children running around. Jameson spotted an ice cream truck that he insisted on going.

"What flavor do you want?", he asked.

"Hmm...", I looked at the menu. "I will have the coffee and cream on a cone, please", I said.

Jameson takes his wallet out; I told him he didn't have to pay since he's the guest, but he insisted.

"I could have paid you know; you already drove out here the least I could do is get your ice cream", I said.

"How about you just make it up by giving me the best tour of Woodbridge?", he responded.

"Well, over there is the dumpster, there's the playground, there's a tree and a squirrel, and there's the river", I jokingly said.

"Wow, you suck as a tour guide", Jameson responded then we both laughed.

We headed towards the wooden bench swing facing the water. We both slowly took a seat and ate our ice cream in silence. I looked over to Jameson when I caught him staring at me.

"What?", I said with a soft laugh.

"Nothing, it's just, it's great to see you Nat", he said.

"Yeah, you were busy the last few weeks of school, so Jake and I didn't get to see you as much. Have you talked to him or seen him?", I asked.

Jameson looked away before responding.

"Not really, I think he's busy with summer work. How about you?", he asked.

"Yeah, we text when we can. He said he wants to hangout", I said.

"Oh", Jameson responded as he went for a bite of his ice cream.

We finished our ice cream, we both put our hands down on the space between us and felt his hand touching mine. We looked at each other and awkwardly pulled away.

"So, anything interesting going on with you?", I asked to break the silence.

"What do you mean?", he asked.

"Any girl or someone special you're talking to?", I said.

"Oh, yeah, no. Not really", he responded.

"How about you? Any guy come around?", he asked.

I thought about asking him his thoughts about Jake and how things were starting to feel different with Jake, but I figured not.

"No, just work. And the occasional middle-aged men that comes in for coffee who calls me, "sweetheart", and tells me that I have a beautiful smile", I jokingly responded.

"You do", he said.

"I do, what?" I looked at Jameson.

"I mean, they're not wrong, you do have a beautiful smile", Jameson responded.

I laughed then turned to look at Jameson when I realized that he's probably not joking. I looked away and put my head down. I can still feel his eyes on me.

"What do you want to see next? I can show you where the post office is where all the chaos happens", I finally said.

"I'll follow your lead", Jameson stood up and offered me his hand to help me up.

We started walking when Jameson found a soccer ball by the bushes. He kicks the ball towards me.

"Well, Miss Natalie Anne let's see those soccer skills", he teased.

I rolled my eyes at him and started to dribble the ball towards the soccer net.

"Just so you know, I was in the states team in middle school so I can't promise that I will take it easy on you, Mr. Williams", I responded.

We played around for a while; I was about to score a goal when I tripped and almost fell. Jameson caught me, he held me in his arms, and we stared into each other's eyes. It felt like a scene from a romantic movie, the sound of the children yelling and people talking disappeared, and I could see was his brown hair and hazel eyes. The sun was shining right on him, his white shirt looked like an aura. Jameson slowly gets closer; I tried standing up but the way he looks made my legs feel weak.

"You found my soccer ball!", said a little boy standing behind Jameson.

We moved away from each other and turned our attention to the boy who apparently owns this soccer ball.

"Here you go buddy", Jameson lightly passed the ball to the kid.

"Well, I think we learned today that you might be the clumsiest person in Woodbridge", Jameson teased.

I chuckled and jokingly punched him in the chest, then we started to walk away.

We didn't say much to each other but quietly walked side-by-side. Knowing that we were in each other's company was enough. Jameson looked at me and slowly grabbed my right hand, before I know it, we were holding hands down the street. I didn't protest, I mean we've held hands and walked arm and arm in the past, so this is nothing new. But this time, it did feel different.

It was almost four in the afternoon, Jameson offered to take me home, so he did. He held the door open for me, I put the window down and let the sun and wind hit my face. I looked over to Jameson, he was focused on the road. Jade might be right, Jameson is hot. His hair was blowing in the wind, he had his sunglasses on and looked like an ad from a car commercial. I smiled and turned to look out the window again.

We finally made it home, Jameson insisted on getting out to help with my door.

"So, I had a great time today. Thanks for being my personal tour-guide", he said.

"I'm so glad you came to visit, I missed hanging out with you", I said as we both hugged each other.

Jameson held me for a while and I did too, we missed each other. I almost didn't want to let go. I slowly pulled away; Jameson kept his hands on my waist as he slowly leaned in closer to my face.

"Hey Nat!", Jade yelled from the front door.

Jameson quickly pulled away and let out a huge sigh.

"Text me when you get home", I said.

"I will", he said.

"And text me more often, stop disappearing on me", I demanded.

"Yes ma'am", Jameson teased and smiled.

Jameson started to walk to his car, he waved to Jade and looked back at me. I started to head towards the front door. I already know that Jade has an entire book of questions especially after what she saw. I turned around and waved bye to Jameson and watched him drive away. I walked pass Jade, who had the most mischievous smile on her face. I smiled back at her and headed up to my room to get changed.

THE REHEARSAL DINNER

I made it to the altar and gave Jake a smile, he took both my hands and held them as if he never wants to let go. The officiator went over the readings, when we can say our vows, and procession again. Saying, "I do", even though it's only our rehearsal made things feel more real. I'm looking at Jake and I know that he's the one I want to spend the rest of my life with. But part of me feels that maybe we should hold off on our wedding. At least until things die down with Jameson. Then again, we have less than twenty-four hours before the real ceremony.

It was finally time for dinner, we all sat at the big table, Jade sat next to me as the maid of honor and Jameson sat at the other end of the table, away from me and Jake. Everyone was having a nice time, conversing with each other, exchanging stories of how they know me and Jake when Jeanine stood up to give a toast.

"Everyone, if you'll spare a moment of your time. I just want to say how happy I am that my son, my only child, found someone who I know will love and cherish him as I have for the rest of his life. As your mother Jake, I was a bit jealous and selfish because I was the first woman you ever loved. But, Natalie, you have been a great addition to our family, and I am extremely delighted to have you as my daughter-in-law. May you have a wonderful marriage and a life full of love. To the bride and groom", she raised her glass.

Jake stood up to give his mother a hug and I followed behind him. Not long after Jade stands up to say her piece.

"I wanted to save my speech tomorrow night, but I figured I'll say a little something. Natalie is the strongest woman and the best friend a girl could ask for. I never had a sister but having you in my life, Nat, has been a blessing, it kind of feels like I have a sister. You've been through a lot from a very young age but every time you have managed to stand tall and follow your heart. Jake, I know that you will take such great care of her, you have found yourself a woman with the biggest heart. And good luck dealing with her mood swings! To the bride and groom", Jade raised her glass for a toast.

I gave Jade a hug, I was fighting the urge to cry. Jake remained standing and kept his glass of champagne in his hands.

"Well, I suppose I'll say a little something. Thank you all for being a part of our day and for sharing this evening with us. I know that it means the world to me and Natalie", Jake said.

"The last few weeks has not been easy", he paused.

My heart stops, is he really going to tell everyone what we've been through the last few weeks??

"I guess in every relationship it's bound to happen when your love and trust for each other will be tested. Natalie and I have been through a lot, I'll be lying if I didn't say that we didn't have doubts for each other. But I think that it's important for relationships to be tested, it shows what you're willing to give someone and how much you're willing to fight for someone, if you know that it's right", Jake continued.

"What I'm trying to say is that after everything and no matter what happens, I will never stop fighting for you, Nat. You will always be my best friend and the person I want to spend the rest of my life with. I love you", he said as he held his hands to help me up.

Jake then kissed me, and everyone cheered. I glanced over at Jameson who slowly turned and walked away. I wanted to follow him, but everyone came over at once to congratulate me and Jake. I watched Jameson walk away with his head low and hands in his pockets.

"Go", Jake whispered.

"What?", I responded.

"Go, he's your best friend too not just mine. Go and get your closure", he said as he gave me a sincere smile.

I smiled back at Jake, gave him a kiss as I walked towards Jameson. I found Jameson sitting alone by the gazebo. I slowly walked over and sat next to him. His head was hanging low, he took a deep breath and acknowledged me by nodding his head. We sat in silence as we both sighed at the same time.

"Do you remember the day you came to Woodbridge?", I said.

Jameson looked at me and nodded his head yes.

"I was thinking about it earlier, actually, right before I walked down the aisle", I started.

"I remember when you showed up, I was really happy to see you. You know, that was the anniversary of my grandmother's death? If you didn't show up, I probably would have stayed home and cried all afternoon", I shared.

"I was thinking about the two chances we could have had", I said.

Jameson looked at me with a confused look on his face.

"I see it now and I'm sorry that I didn't before. I remember the moment when I thought you were going to kiss me when I tripped over a soccer ball, the second time when you dropped me off, but Jade interrupted us", I let out a fake laugh as I looked into his eyes.

"Jameson, I really am sorry. I'm sorry that I didn't see it then. Truth be told after that day I thought that maybe you had feelings for me too", I said.

"Too?", he finally said.

"I had feelings for you especially when we first met but at the time I thought for sure that you only saw me as a friend and I didn't want to ruin anything", I confessed.

"I remember calling Jade on the very first day of school and told her about you. About this guy that I met in class and was nothing but nice to me all day. After that I looked forward to lunch every day because I got to see you and spend time with you. At one point, I thought that maybe you had feelings for me too but then I remember you said that you met someone, so I backed off. Then Jake and I spent more time together and I fell in love with him", I said.

Jameson was quiet for a while, now that he knows that I had feelings for him too I feel even dumber that we're sitting in this gazebo, less than twenty-four hours before I marry his best friend.

"Nat, why do you think I drove all the way out to Woodbridge that day?", he said.

"I remember you saying that July 6th is your grandmother's death anniversary. I guess I just didn't want you to be alone. But I drove over an hour to see you because…well, I was going to ask you out", Jameson continued.

"Then when I got there, I asked for you. Jade thought that I was Jake, she made a comment about how you and Jake had been talking so she thought that I was him. So, I didn't, I didn't ask you out, I didn't ask you to be mine", he confessed.

"That girl that I told you about, that was you. I was too much of a coward to say anything and I wish that I had the nerve to ask you out then. I missed my chances and I know that", he continued.

He clears his throat and looks away. I could see the sadness in his eyes.

"I wanted to tell you that day that I have never met someone like you. That being around you, being with you was refreshing because I could be myself. I wanted to tell you that every day I looked forward to seeing your smile, to hear your voice, and to see you come out of your shell each day", Jameson paused and looks at me.

"I wanted to tell you that day that I have never felt love until I met you", his voice faded.

We sat in silence; we could hear everyone cheering and having a great time inside while we sat next to each other. Sitting next to him hurt, not because I'm angry at him, I don't think I am anymore, but it hurts knowing that we both have our own fair share of regrets.

"I wanted to kiss you. I wanted to see what it would be like but every time I tried, I got nervous, so I didn't", he confessed.

"I want you to be happy, I want you to live a happy life with Jake. He loves you and I've seen the way he cares for you. I don't regret standing next to him tomorrow. The only thing I regret is the pain I've caused you over the last few weeks. I'm happy for you both Nat, I truly am", he reassured me.

"Are you going to stick around after tomorrow?", I asked.

Jameson was quiet, he held my hand, but he didn't bother to look at me.

"I'm moving to Colorado in two days", he finally said.

"Oh", that was all that I could say.

Tears started to roll down my face, the thought of not having my best friend hurt.

"Will you stay in touch?", I asked.

"I…I'm moving to have a fresh start", he responded.

"So…tomorrow's it, then? After tomorrow I won't hear from you or see you anymore?", I asked, my voice was shaking as I tried not to cry in front of him.

"Yeah, tomorrow's *it*", he said.

I couldn't fight the tears anymore and started to cry even harder. I put my hands over my face as I turned my body away from him as if it would make me invincible. I wiped the tears off my face then looked in his direction and watched as tears quietly rolled down his face.

"This isn't fair", I finally said.

"You're my best friend, you're the reason I got through my first year of college. How am I supposed to go from being so close to you and to never seeing you again?", I said.

"I'm sorry that our timing was never right. I want you to walk down the aisle tomorrow and marry Jake. I want you to have a good life, to have a family of your own, you're going to be a great wife to him", he said as he turned towards me.

Jameson lifted my head with his hands and forced me to look him in the eyes. He brushed my hair off my face and gave me a smile. He looked at me as if he's trying to memorize every part of me as if he didn't want to forget what I looked like. Jameson started nodding his head then slowly stood up. He looked at me again, it felt like it really is the last time we'll ever see each other. I wanted to protest and convince him to stay but that would be selfish of me. I heard footsteps coming from behind me, it was Jake. I watched Jameson walk slowly towards Jake, he offered his hand to Jake, then they hugged each other.

"Promise me that you'll take good care of her, alright?", Jameson said to Jake.

"Always", Jake responded.

"I'll see you tomorrow" Jameson said as he walked away.

I couldn't stop myself from crying, Jake kneeled in front of me. He grabbed my hands and pulled me towards him to comfort me.

"He's leaving…for good", I said to Jake.

"I know", Jake said as he continued to rub my back and hold me in his arms.

THE BRIDE

It felt like I didn't get any sleep at all last night. Jake slept at the hotel about five minutes from the venue and I stayed at an Airbnb with the girls. I always pictured this moment to be different. I always thought that I'd lose sleep from being too excited and anxiety. Instead, I woke up with heartache after last night, and instead of thinking about my groom, I'm thinking about someone else. I didn't want to move; I couldn't help but start crying when I try to look back at everything that has happened between Jameson and me.

Jade knocked on my door with a tray of bagel and mimosa.

"Happy wedding day!!", Jade cheered.

Then she paused when she saw that I have been crying. She closed the door behind her and set the tray on the dresser by the door then came running towards me.

"Oh, Nat, what's wrong? It's perfectly normal to feel nervous, it's your wedding day after all", she tried to comfort me.

I wipe the tears off my face and tried to pull myself together. Before I could gather the courage to tell Jade about last night, she grabs my right hand and let out a sigh.

"Do you want to tell me where you went off to last night?", she asked.

I took a deep breath and looked at Jade, but my vision was a little too blurry from the tears that kept coming right back.

"After Jake made the toast, I saw Jameson walk out…Jake told me to go follow him and get my closure, so I did", I started.

"I followed Jameson outside and we talked. I told him how I remember the day he came to surprise me at the café, how I felt stupid that I didn't see it then",

"He told me that he's moving to Colorado in two days, after today I'll never see him again. I messed it all up, Jade, I really did", I cried.

Jade held me in her arms then slowly she let me go.

"Nat", Jade said.

"Do you want to marry Jake today?", she asked.

I couldn't look at Jade in the eyes. I want to marry Jake, I do. I've loved him for the last five years and I have been looking forward to this day up until a few weeks ago. I paused and glanced over at my wedding dress that's hanging on the closet door.

"I...I do. I don't know", I continued to cry.

"Since the day we got engaged I looked forward to this day. I was supposed to wake up happy, excited, drinking mimosas, and eager to get ready but I don't feel any of that. Not anymore at least", I confessed.

"Then don't", Jade said softly.

"What?", I asked as if I didn't hear her the first time.

"Then don't marry him, Nat, you know that I love you and I want nothing but the best for you, for you to be happy for the rest of your life. But, if you walk down that aisle today and you say, *I do*, knowing that you don't want to get married then how fair do you think that is for Jake? I've watched you the last month go on and on about Jake then Jameson then Jake, it's enough already Nat. You're not hurting yourself, you're hurting Jake", Jade said.

She's telling the truth, Jade's the only one who can be this honest with me. What am I doing? What am I going to do?

"You know that I love you more than anything and I will always take your side but not this time. I think that you've made a choice", Jade then said as she gave me a kiss on the top of my head.

Jade walked out and closed the door behind her. I continued to cry as I stared at my wedding dress. I slowly walked towards it and closed my eyes, every time I picture myself wearing it, I don't see Jake. I see Jameson waiting at the end of the aisle. I see myself walking happily and saying my vows and walking out as a wife. But not to Jake, I don't even see his face anymore, all I see is Jameson. I see his dark hair, brown eyes, his smile, and the way he looks at me. I see the time at the park when I almost fell and he caught me in his arms, the time when he dropped me off and we almost kissed. Then I see him walking in the rain towards me, the way he looked when he first confessed his feelings for me, the way he was hurting, and the way he kissed me.

I slowly opened my eyes, Jade was right, what am I doing? I was about to come out of the room when Jeanine slowly opened the door.

"There she is, our bride", Jeanine said as she went in for a hug.

The hairstylist and makeup crew were here, Jeanine invited them into my room and showed them where to setup their stuff. I stood there almost frozen. The photographer followed behind the makeup lady then read the list of events that I had asked her to capture for today. I could hear Jeanine talking to everyone, but I couldn't focus, everything was starting to sound muffled.

"Nat?", Jeanine said. I then realized that her hand was on my shoulder.

"Honey, why don't you go get showered and I'll bring you something to eat so you can start getting ready?", Jeanine guided me towards the bathroom.

I stood in the bathroom, still frozen, I was starting to have a hard time breathing. I heard someone knocking on the door.

"Nat?", Jade whispered as she slowly opened the bathroom door.

"Here I'll set your stuff up, go brush your teeth", she said.

Jade turned the shower on for me and laid a towel on the counter. Jade then hung up a white satin robe that said, "bride", on the back.

"Are you okay?", she asked.

I nodded my head yes and started to get in the shower. As soon as the water touched my head, I started crying even harder than it was earlier. I slowly sat down and covered my mouth with my hands so Jeanine and her crew wouldn't hear me crying. I was ready but maybe I was about to make the wrong decision. It hurt to think that for two minutes I considered leaving Jake at the altar. What kind of a person am I? After that it made me feel that I don't deserve Jake even more. What kind of life am I going to give him if I'm not a hundred percent into it? And what about Jameson? He had…we both had our chances, but we missed it. I found someone who was brave enough to take my hand and tell me that he loved me, am I really willing to let Jake go for someone who was not strong enough to fight for me then?

I kept asking myself questions until I found myself calm enough that I could finally come out of the shower. Slowly, I dried myself off, and got dressed. I put the robe on and looked at myself in the mirror. I took a deep breath then opened the door. Just as I expected, Jeanine was talking to Jade's mom and the girls. Everyone looked at me with tears in their eyes.

"Calm down ladies, this is just the robe", I said jokingly then everyone came closer for a group hug.

Everyone was finally dressed and ready to go. I was sitting in the room by myself in my robe with my makeup and hair done. Sam came in with a white box and a letter,

"Take you time", she said.

I looked at the box and it had a number 2 on it, so I figured that I'm supposed to read the letter first.

> *Nat,*
>
> *I remember the day that we met. You were wearing a dusty blue dress, pair of white vans, your hair was down, and applied very light makeup. I remember walking up to you and I knew immediately that I had to get to know you more. Every day for the first two years of college I thought of you and how meeting you has made every single day better. I think since day one I always pictured the day that I would ask you to be my girlfriend and then to be my wife. We have built a life together ever since and I wouldn't have it any other way.*
>
> *I want you to know that my love for you is real. No matter what after today, no matter what choice you make, I want you to know that I'll support it and I'll continue to love you even if you don't choose me. I'll always be here for you, Nat. At the end of the day, all I want is for you to be happy.*
>
> *-Jake.*

I read the letter three times, what does he mean by, "no matter what choice you make"? I opened the white box, and it was a snow globe with a picture of Jake, Jameson, and I at the freshman year bonfire. I still remember that night clear as day. I took the snow globe out of the box and placed it on my chest. Part of me knows that the pain is because no matter what decision I make I'll end up hurting one of the most important people in my life. I tried not to cry so much so I didn't ruin my makeup. I stood up and walked towards my dress, three times I looked back and forth between my dress, the letter, and our picture.

"Okay girls now stand over here by the arch way, here she comes!", the photographer announced.

I came around the corner, in my dress, veil, and bouquet in my hands. I looked up and met eyes with Jade. She had her hands clasped together under her chin with happy tears building up in her eyes. Before Jade could come up to me, Jeanine gave me the biggest hug and cried. I tried not to cry, I took a deep breath and put a smile on my face.

"So, you made a choice", Jade whispered as she fixed my hair.

"Yeah, you were right", I said.

"Is this what you want?", Jade asked.

I paused and looked around,

"It is", I said.

The photographer then took some pictures of us in the living room and back porch where no one could see us. Everyone around me felt like they were running around, moving too fast. I started to feel a heavy weight on my chest and slowly leaned back. Jeanine then came around the corner and told not to lean on the wall because it might ruin my hair and wrinkly my dress.

Slowly the girls started to line up the door to get to the garden where we're having the ceremony. The weather today was perfect, the sun is out but not too hot either. For a moment I caught myself feeling excited and happy. Then my stomach drops as I headed for the door; the wedding coordinator was standing by the door waiting to escort me out. I stopped and took deep breaths; I closed my eyes…

JUST A MEMORY

"So where are you from?", Jameson asked.

"Woodbridge, New Jersey. How about you?", I said.

"Philly, so we're neighbors", he joked.

Jameson and I walked together to the math building since we have our next class together. I'm looking around and it's pretty easy to tell who's in their first year and who's not. I noticed that he walks with both hands in his pockets, or maybe he's just trying to be awkward. Which made me self-conscious of what I'm doing with my hands as we continued to walk.

"So, why did you decide to come here? Scholarship? Friends? Boyfriend?", he asked.

"Oh, yea I had a scholarship and it's close enough to home", I responded.

"So, no boyfriend then?", he jokingly asked.

"Ha! No, I haven't been with anyone…I mean not since last year", I responded nervously. I could feel my cheeks turning red.

"Why'd you breakup?", he asked.

"It just wasn't right, he wanted to move to Chicago, and I wasn't ready to make a move that big yet, so we broke up after we got our acceptance letters last year", I explained.

"Well, I'm glad you didn't go to Chicago", he said.

"I haven't dated anyone since 10th grade which come to think of it, I don't really think that counts for anything", he said.

"How come? I mean you seem pretty sociable", I said.

"Just didn't feel like it, it's just me, my mom, and little brother, so I had to work. I didn't have much time to hang around other people", he explained.

Before I know it, we were already at the entrance of the building, we looked around once we made it inside. I'm glad Jameson is here because I'd probably get lost...again.

We found our classroom, Jameson and I found two seats towards the back and sat next to each other again.

"Are you okay?", he whispered.

"Huh?", I turned towards him.

"You're picking on your nails and you're shaking your legs", he said.

"Oh, yeah, no. I'm okay", I whispered back.

He's pretty observant, I do pick on my nails when I'm nervous. The professor then made an announcement that he's going to break us up into small groups so we can get to know other people in our class. He assigned us number from 1 to 4, I happen to be number 2 and Jameson is 3, which means that we won't be in the same group, *great*.

I headed towards the left side of the room and Jameson stayed where we were, I slowly approached my group. Everyone seems so much more mature looking than me, I mean, I'm not calling them old, but I just never thought about doing my makeup or dressing up like most girls my age. I like to stay comfortable and simple so by the end of the day all I have to do is kick my shoes off and turn on shows to watch. I tried to look behind me to see how Jameson was doing but he seemed to be taking over the group. Everyone was in his group was laughing at what he was saying. There two girls in his group who both seems to have their eyes on him.

"And you?", said a student.

"Huh?", I asked.

"Your name", the girl to my right said.

"Oh, I'm Natalie", I responded then sank into my seat.

Everyone in my group seems to find something in common with each other, they really didn't ask me anything other than my name. I looked around and noticed that everyone was talking to each other as if they've known each other for years. I looked at the time and noticed that it was finally time to leave, *thank God*.

The rest of my group stood and walked towards the door together, I was left by myself. I stood there for a minute, awkwardly waiting for Jameson. But what am I thinking? It looks like he finally found a group plus he has two girls in his group who are dressed way nicer than I do. I quietly started to head towards the door. I made it out to the hallway and realized that I'm back to being Natalie, just Natalie. I mean at least I shared my name twice so far this morning. I finally found the exit door; I took a deep breath once I finally made it out. My next class is not until 2pm so I guess I have time to grab something quick to eat in the comfort of my own room.

I stopped at a grab and go spot in the cafeteria building then headed towards my dorm room.

"Natalie! Hey! Nat!", I heard someone yelling my name.

I turned to find that it was Jameson. He told me that he had been trying to find me since class ended. I told him that I didn't want to interrupt him, so I left. Jameson introduced me to his friends, Jake aka peanut free guy also his childhood best friend, Ty, and Jason. Jameson then asked if I wanted to join them for lunch. I looked down at my sad ham and cheese sandwich and apple, I looked at him then behind me towards the dorm rooms then finally agreed to join them.

"We'll be right there guys", Jameson said to his friends.

"I'm sorry", he apologized.

"For what?", I asked.

"For ditching you in class and realizing that I put you on the spot just now. If you have other lunch plans you don't have to force yourself to join us", he said.

"Oh, no it's fine. You don't have to apologize", I responded.

"I also realized that I forgot to ask for your number, you know so we can hang out or schoolwork stuff", he said as he handed me his phone.

"Schoolwork stuff?", I jokingly said.

I put my number on his phone then he sent me a text right away.

Hi Ms. Natalie Anderson

"I'm standing right here", I laughed.

"I know but I wanted to make sure you didn't give me a fake number", he joked.

He guided me towards the spot under the tree where his friends were waiting. Jameson and his friends convinced me to come out to some bonfire later tonight for all first-year students, I guess I have to go since I told them I'll see them later. I went back to my room and finally I was on my own again. I called Jade then we talked for a while about our first day. She was really excited when I told her that the first "friend" I made is a boy.

After Jade and I hung up the phone I planned on taking a nap but instead I spent the next thirty-minutes staring at my clothes and realized that I have nothing bonfire attire. Ugh, I decided to go classic and picked out a pair of jeans and my black long-sleeved shirt like Jade suggested. I finally went to rest my eyes before my next class and bonfire festivities later, but I can't help but think about Jameson. He has been so kind and patient with me all day. It almost felt as if we've known each other for years.

After I got back Jess was already gone so I decided to start getting ready. I grabbed my phone to see if Jameson had texted me, but he hasn't, did he forget he invited me to come hangout with them tonight? The last thing I want is to show up and he doesn't remember who I am and why he invited me. I decided to give myself a minute and let the negative thoughts pass before I gathered the courage to make my way towards the front door. I noticed that every single freshman is going to be at this bonfire, and it looks like everyone found someone to hangout with. I stopped and looked around to see if I could spot Jameson and his group. I started walking towards them when Jake called my name and waved his arms in the air.

THE CEREMONY

I opened my eyes and took a step out the door to get in the van so I can hide from all the guests and Jake. I was about to get in the van when noticed a tall figure in a gray suit who was slowly walking up towards the van, towards me, it was Jameson. I asked Irene to give us a minute, I handed Irene my bouquet and asked for her to put it in the van then I started walking towards Jameson. His eyes, they look so sad, I could tell that he probably didn't sleep too well either.

"Hey", I greeted him.

"You look...you look amazing, Nat", he said in almost complete shock.

Then I realized that this is his first time seeing me in my wedding dress just thirty-minutes before I have to walk down the aisle. We stood there in silence, I wanted to hug him, to tell him that everything is okay, I want to tell him that I wish we could turn back time, but we can't. And most of all, I want to tell him that I choose Jake.

"What are you doing here?", I finally asked.

"I don't really have a reason, I just wanted to see you off", he said.

"Shouldn't you be with the guys right now?", I asked.

"Yeah, I mean, they're all where they're supposed to be and it won't take me long to get there", he responded.

"Okay...I do have to go", I said softly.

Suddenly I felt the tears start to build in my eyes, so I looked away and tried to act okay. I gave Jameson a smile and turned towards the van when he gently grabbed my arm. I turned back to look at him.

"Jameson, don't", I whispered.

"I just wanted to say that I'm happy for you, you're making the right choice. All I ever wanted was for you to be happy. I wanted you to know that I've told Jake that I'll be leaving right after the ceremony", he said.

"I told him that it's bad enough that I'll be in the pictures from the ceremony, so I don't want to ruin the rest of your memories too", he followed.

"You're not ruining anything, you're a part of this day because you're important to us", I told him.

"I know but I think that the memories we shared is good enough and I've caused enough chaos during this time", he explained.

"Are you really leaving? For good?", I asked, my voice shakes.

"I came here to tell you that I'm glad we met, and I will *always* wish you the best...even from afar", he responded.

I let a tear escape and finally gave him a hug, it was brief but long enough that I hope he knows how sorry I am for everything. It was long enough that it felt like an entire weight was taken off my shoulders. It was long enough that I was able to say my goodbyes because in thirty-minutes I know that it will be the last time I'll see him.

"Don't ruin your makeup, you do look amazing, *Miss* Natalie Ann Anderson", he squeezed my hands, smiled, and walked away.

I wiped the tears off my face as I watched him walk further away. Watching him take each step made it feel like my heart was being torn into pieces, one step at a time.

I finally started to turn towards the van and finally was able to get in. I looked at Irene hoping that she didn't see or hear any of that.

Slowly we pulled into the area where I'm supposed to get dropped off, we had time, so I stayed in the van while I watched the guests walk in. I realized that I don't recognize some people we had invited, I mean, some of them are Jeanine's old colleagues who met Jake when he was born. Slowly, the staff members started to stand by the entry way, my heart started beating fast again, I started picking on my nails.

Part of me didn't want to get out and walk down the aisle because it means that after this, I won't see Jameson again. Then another part of me feels anxious and excited to finally meet Jake at the altar. I've been dreaming about this very moment since I was a little girl, like any girl, we all dream of our wedding day, hoping to live a fairytale. That moment when you finally get to put on a long white dress, a veil, and tiara, then you get to live your happily ever after with your prince. But this doesn't feel quite like a fairytale, it's like a long dream that started off with a prince on a white horse just to end with a cruel witch waiting for you to fail down the road. That's exactly how I feel, I feel like a witch has casted a spell on me and made sure that I don't get to live my happily ever after.

Slowly everyone settled in their seats, my girls started to walk down the aisle, followed by the ring bearer and flower girl. Then it was finally my turn, Irene came to open the car door and helped me out. My legs felt like jelly and my hands were shaking. I took a deep breath as I started to head towards the entrance and waited for my queue from the pianist. I decided to walk down the aisle to, "To Make You Feel My Love" by Adele. I thought it was fitting, all these years, Jake has been nothing but kind and loving. He has sacrificed so much to give us, me, a good life. Then my time finally came…

I came around the corner and tried my best not to look at the guests too much. I hate when people look at me, it makes me uncomfortable. Then I finally looked up and found Jake standing at the end of the altar, I started to tear up the moment my eyes laid on him. He looked perfect. Jake was smiling as he wiped his tears off his face. I couldn't help but look over at Jameson. To my surprise he seemed fine. His hands were in his pockets as he stared at me with a smile on his face. I smiled back.

Then my heart started to sink, I wish that he can hear what's going on in my head. I wish that he can hear me say how sorry I am that our timing was never right and that I never wanted for him to move away. In less than an hour, he'll be gone. Jameson said that he doesn't want to be in the wedding party pictures because he wants me and Jake to remember this day with nothing but happy memories. But how can I be happy? When I look back on my wedding day and everything leading up to it, I'll always remember how I didn't realize that part of me wanted him too.

Slowly I made my way down the aisle and when I finally reached the end, I handed my bouquet to Jade then Jake walked over to offer me his hands as we stood under the arbor. We held hands as we stared into each other's eyes, I took a deep breath as the officiator started to welcome everyone and start off with a prayer. We closed our eyes and bowed our heads down; I opened my eyes and saw Jameson staring right at me. "Oh, dear Lord, please help me get through this", I said to myself.

"We are gathered here today to celebrate and witness as Jake and Natalie become husband and wife. To celebrate their love for one another and for many years to come", the officiator started.

Then it was time for us to share our vows, Jake started off with his vows first.

"Nat, our paths crossed a little over six years ago. From the moment I saw you to the moment when I finally found the courage to ask you out, part of me always knew that you were the one", he started.

"We have been tested time and time again, but you never gave up on me and I promise that I will never give up on you. I promise to be the best husband I can be, to be supportive, to love you, take care of you, and most of all protect you. You have always been the person I know I can trust, and I know that we will share our forever with honesty and truth. I love you".

My heart was beating as fast as a hamster running in spinning wheel. Jade handed me my vow which I wrote last night. After hearing Jake's vows, I don't think I can read what I wrote because it doesn't do his love justice. I cleared my throat, closed my eyes, and took a deep breath.

"I'll be honest, I wrote my vows last night", I started then heard everyone laughing including Jake.

"But I don't think what I wrote is enough nor does it justify the man that you have been to me", I continued as I took the piece of paper and crumbled it in my hands.

"Jake, you have been patient with me even when you had every reason not to be. You've taken care of me, provided for us, and showed me what love is", I paused, I started picking on my nails as I kept my head low and nervously continued my vow.

"You've made me laugh when I thought my world was crumbling down, you've taught me to be confident in my skin, and most of all you've taught me what commitment truly is", I paused again then looked up. I went to continue on but could not help but look right at Jameson as he was also staring at me.

"We've shared a lot of memories together that I will forever cherish, and I want you to know that I am grateful for all of those memories. I'm grateful that a man like you walked into my life and made it ten times better. You've helped me come out of my shell and be the person that I am now", I said as I took another look at Jameson and started to tear up.

"I am not perfect and will never be perfect. But I do promise to love you and to be the best wife I can be", I finally ended.

Finally, it was time to exchange rings.

"Jake, please repeat after me", the officiator instructed.

"With this ring, I, Jake, promise to love you, cherish you, and honor you, till death parts us", the officiator said.

"With this ring, I, Jake, promise to love you, cherish you, and honor you, till death parts us", Jake repeated as he slipped my ring into my finger.

Then it was my turn...

"With this ring, I, Natalie, promise to love you, cherish you, and honor you, till death parts us", I repeated then it was my turn to give Jake his ring.

"Jake, do you take Natalie to be your wife? Do you promise to love her, honor her, cherish her, and protect her through all the ups and downs, till death parts you? If so, please say I do", said the officiator.

Jake looked me in the eyes as he said, "I do".

"Natalie, do you take Jake to be your husband? Do you promise to love him, honor him, cherish him, and protect him through all the ups and downs, till death parts you? If so, please say I do", the officiator said to me.

I froze, slowly I let my hands slip out of Jake's hands, I watched as the smile on his face slowly went away. I could hear the murmuring from the guests. I looked pass Jake and made eye contact with Jameson, who looked very anxious.

"Natalie?", the officiator said my name once again.

I looked at the officiator and took deep breaths. I looked at Jake in the eyes again.

"Sorry, yes, I do", I finally responded.

I looked over at Jake's mother who looked relieved, I noticed that Jake was still staring at me with a concerned look on his face.

"And now, by the power vested in me, I now pronounce you husband and wife. Jake you may now kiss your bride",

Jake took a step closer to me as we shared our first kiss as husband and wife. Everyone started cheering as they congratulated us on our new adventure together. Deep inside I was happy and sad at the same time, part of me still doesn't know if this is the right decision or if it's time for me to let my fantasy go. Slowly, Jake and I started to walk down the aisle together, everything happened too fast.

"Hi, Mrs. Natalie Andrews", Jake whispered to me as we stood by end of the aisle, he gave me another kiss.

"Hi, husband", I responded with a smile.

We were instructed by Irene and the photographer to wait for the crowd to leave before we headed by the garden to take our pictures. I turned towards our wedding party and immediately noticed that one of them is missing. I don't know when and how but it looks like this time he's gone. My heart started to sink, I didn't want to make it too obvious that I was looking for him, but I couldn't help but turn my head every now and then to see if he'll come back. We started heading towards the garden with the rest of our bridal party. I decided to check for the last time, but he was nowhere to be found. I guess this is goodbye.

I smiled as I nodded my head. He's right, this is the right choice. I hope that someday he finds the one who will love him and not waste his time. I hope he knows that despite everything that happened this past month that I could never hate him. I hope he knows that I will always love him from afar. I hope he knows that I wish him nothing but the best.

WISH YOU WERE HERE

THE ONE

One by one we followed in line as we walked down the aisle. I watched as the bridesmaids made their way followed by the ringbearer and flower girl. Then the officiator finally instructed everyone to stand and turn towards the bride. I couldn't help but smile as she came around the corner, she's perfect. Her long white dress, veil, and the perfect smile on her face, I couldn't be happier. Every memory that we've shared from the day we met started flooding back. She deserves a happily ever after, she deserves to be loved and honored in every way.

She finally reached the altar when we made eye contact then slowly, he walked towards her and offered his hands. I stood behind Jake while the officiator started the ceremony. Looking at her hurt but I knew that I wouldn't be able to make her as happy. Listening to them share their vows broke my heart into tiny pieces one word at a time. I wish that it was me she was holding hands with right now, I wish it was me that get to spend the rest of my life with her. I tried to keep myself together, part of me wanted to yell, "stop", and ask her to run away with me but that wouldn't be fair to her and him. So, I continued to stand and accepted that she will never be mine.

I watched them exchange rings, I watched the way her brown eyes sparkled, and the way her smile can light up any room.

"Natalie, do you take Jake to be your husband? Do you promise to love him, honor him, cherish him, and protect him through all the ups and downs, till death parts you? If so, please say I do", the officiator said.

She froze, she didn't say a word, the look on her face broke me. What is she doing? Then our eyes locked, I couldn't help but be concerned, is she going to say no? Is she going to take my hands and run away together? No, she wouldn't do that. I smiled at her to let her know that

I was serious when I told her that this is the right decision for her. That she's better off with him even though it hurt.

"Sorry, yes, I do", she finally said.

Then they shared their first kiss as husband and wife and walked down the aisle together. Tears started to fill my eyes, but I kept on smiling and clapped. This was it; she's gone. I let the other groomsmen walk ahead of me then slowly I followed behind the guests as they all pile to walk to the reception hall. I took one more look at her, she looked so happy, I watched her hug and kiss him.

"Goodbye, Natalie", I said to myself.

DUSTY BLUE DRESS

I walked into the lecture hall with my eyes half closed. Most freshmen are dressed to impress considering it's the first day of school. I kept walking up the steps until I could find a seat that was far enough that I could still see the screen to take notes. I watched everyone find their seat until the professor walked in. I enjoy people watching, I've always wondered what is going on inside someone's head when they wake up in the morning. Why did they decide to wear what they're wearing? What does the world look like from their perspective?

I pulled my phone out until it was time for class when I looked up and noticed a very anxious, nervous, and shy girl. She was wearing a dusty blue dress with white shoes, her brown hair was perfectly straight, the way she anxiously looked for a seat until she noticed the empty one next to me. Suddenly I felt my heart beating fast and the way I couldn't stop looking at her. I caught myself before she could, I casually adjusted myself in my seat then the professor walked in. He was wearing a long white button up shirt, khaki-colored pants, brown shoes, with a black brief case in his hands. Everyone immediately stopped talking as we watched him write his name on the board, *Dr. Charles Goldin.*

"Good morning, everyone, welcome", Dr. Goldin greeted us.

"Good morning", we responded in unison.

"I won't be doing this every day; you will find a sign-in sheet by the door when you walk in. Saves me time from taking attendance for a class of 80 students. But for today I will be calling your name so please kindly say, here", he instructed us.

Dr. Goldin started to take attendance,

"Natalie Anderson?", he called.

No response.

"Is there a Miss Natalie Anderson, here?", he called again.

I realized noticed her notebook, "Natalie", was written on the front page. I gently nudged her and pointed forward to let her know that her name was being called.

"Oh sorry, here!", she finally responded.

She sank into her seat, and I noticed that her face suddenly turned red. I could tell that she felt uncomfortable and embarrassed, especially in a classroom full of strangers. I decided to talk to her and be a friend. That's what college is about, right? To meet people and make friends.

"You should really pay more attention, *Miss Anderson*", I finally said to her.

She looked at me and smiled. I pointed out her planner and how well prepared she was, me on the other hand, came with a pen, notebook, and a folder. She was explaining things to me but it's like I couldn't hear what she was saying. The way she talked, the way she cared for her things, and the way her eyes looked caught me off guard. Shit, college started twenty minutes ago, and I think I may have already fallen for her.

Before I knew it class was over, I quickly packed up my things to keep up with her. I looked up and she was gone then I spotted her a couple steps down. I tried to fight my way through the crowd, why do people walk so damn slow?! I finally made it out then saw her standing while she looked at a piece of paper.

"Hey, I figured we could walk together since I have the same class", I approached her.

"I know the way", I said to her.

I tried my best to stay beside her but without making myself come out as a creep, is that what I'm doing? Am I creeping her out? We started talking and I learned that she's from Woodbridge, she's an only child, and she was an honor student. Most importantly I learned that she's single. Every time she spoke, I couldn't help but look at her, the way that the sun hit her, I noticed how brown her eyes were and the way she looked effortlessly beautiful. I couldn't help but wonder how guys have never noticed her. It sounds cliché I know but she looked like an angel.

I started thinking about how I can spend time with her outside of our classes, would it be too weird if I asked her for her number now?

No, that'll be too weird, I need to wait for the right timing. Before we knew it, after ten minutes we finally made it to the great math hall. We found two seats together, I assumed that she wanted to sit with me. I hope she doesn't feel forced to sit next to me.

Same as our first class, we started with teacher introductions, attendance, went over the syllabus, then we were broken into small groups. Sadly, Natalie and I were not in the same group. I watched her nervously approach her group, she sat down and introduced herself, but it didn't look like she could get a word in with the rest of her group. I wanted to walk over and tell everyone how amazing of a person she is, but then I've only known her for an hour and a half at this point.

I started engaging with my group and every chance I could get I would look over at Natalie to see how she was doing, she seemed like she was trying her best, but she doesn't seem like the type of person who will talk about herself for hours. I think that's what attracted me the most about her, usually, in my experience girls will try to compete with each other and talk about themselves. But not her, she's so humble and down to earth.

By the time our group finally said our goodbyes, she was gone! I panicked and quickly grabbed my stuff while I looked for her, but she was nowhere to be found. I guess I'll see her in class on Wednesday. I couldn't help but relive the moment I saw her. I kept my eyes out for her in case she's lost somewhere.

"Hey! Jay!", I heard a familiar voice call me.

I turned and found Jake.

"What's up man", I said to Jake.

"My morning has been boring, if I have to introduce myself one more time and share my favorite food I might drop out", he jokingly said.

"How's your morning going?", he asked.

"It's alright, not bad actually", I responded.

Jake has been my best friend since we were kids, we practically grew up together. Jake transferred to my school when we were in grade school. I remember seeing this little boy sitting at the peanut free table, poor guy had no idea that it was a peanut free table, so I joined him and told him that I was allergic too. But I wasn't, I just felt bad because the other kids were making fun of him. After that we have been inseparable, his family welcomed me with open arms when I would come over to spend the night. My mom is a nurse and works nightshifts a lot so when she had to work overnight, she would drop me off at Jake's and we would spend all night playing games, pretending we were soldiers until her mom would come and yell at us. He's my family, he's the reason I decided to give college a shot, I wasn't planning to go to school but Jake talked me into it and I'm glad that I listened.

"Why are you smiling like that?", he teased.

"What?", I quickly wiped the smile off my face.

"Did you meet a girl?", Jake guessed.

"Actually...yes, I did. We have calculus and physics together so", I shared.

"So, this is why you agreed on coming here? For girls", Jake teased again.

"Her name's Natalie, she's real sweet. I'm just trying to make friends, so I don't have to spend every minute with your face", I teased back.

We started walking back towards the dining hall to grab a quick lunch, Ty and Jason were sitting at a picnic table when we finally found them.

"Hey what's up guys", I greeted.

Ty and Jason were in our orientation group, and it happens that they're also roommates who lives across the hall from us. Ty was talking when I saw a familiar dusty blue dress, I found her!

"I'll be right back", as I rushed towards Natalie.

"Hey Nat! Natalie!", I called for her.

She looked like she was about to head back to her room and eat alone.

"I'm sorry", I apologized.

"For what?", she asked.

"For ditching you in class", I explained.

"Oh, no it's fine. You don't have to apologize", she responded.

"I also realized that I forgot to ask for your number, you know so we can hang out or schoolwork stuff", I said then handed her my phone.

"Schoolwork stuff?", she jokingly said.

She puts her number on my phone, and I quickly put my phone in my pocket.

"My friends and I are having lunch over there if you want to join us", I offered.

She didn't respond right away, she looked pass me and saw Ty and Jason laughing.

"I know I'm putting you on the spot, but I promise they're harmless", I said, almost sounding desperate.

"No, I mean yes, I'll join you", she said.

"You must be Miss Natalie", Jake came up behind me and shook her hand.

"I'm Jake", he introduced himself.

"Yeah, remember the peanut free guy", I joked.

Natalie then joined us for lunch, Ty and Jason introduced themselves. I sat across the table from her. I couldn't help but watch her, again, not in a creepy way. The way she laughed at every joke that came out of Ty and Jason, her smile was the best thing I've ever seen. I realized that I haven't stopped smiling all day since I met her. Maybe this is destiny.

Lunch was finally over, I told Natalie about the freshmen bonfire this evening and hope that she'll come. She started to walk away when I pulled my phone out and sent her a text,

Hi Ms. Natalie Anderson

STARTING OVER

After the ceremony, I quietly stood behind the guests, I watched her from afar while she greeted everyone and shared hugs with her new husband. I decided to take it all in, her smile, her existence, her everything, this is it. Slowly I made my way towards the parking lot, I took the keys out of my pocket and got in my car. As soon as I started the car, it felt that a bag of bricks just hit me right in the chest. This is the right thing to do, she doesn't need me to keep messing with her head. She deserves to be loved and happy, if I could turn back time, I wish that I was the one in the suit, I wish that I was the one she's making memories with right now.

I reflected on the memories that we shared, how quickly we became close and how I fell for her. I reflected on how many opportunities I had but I didn't say or do anything. I wish that I was a bigger man and was able to tell her exactly how I felt from the beginning. But I was too afraid, I was afraid that I'd push her away. I closed my eyes and every moment that we shared all came in a flash. I want to hug her one last time, but it won't do us any good and who am I to ruin this day for her. I've done enough, I can't put her through more pain, I hated seeing her cry and upset.

Before I drove away, I decided to delete her number from my phone. Unfollowed her on every social media. If I'm starting over, I need to start now. If I'm moving half a country away then I need to let everything go, right here, right now. Maybe someday I'll see her again and we can laugh about everything. Someday when I see her again, I hope I can hear her laugh again, to see her smile, and listen to her talk. I took a deep breath and started driving. I made my peace, I love you Natalie, I always will.

www.ingramcontent.com/pod-product-compliance
Lightning Source LLC
Chambersburg PA
CBHW020149180626
46810CB00004B/1800